THE X-FILES
x-posed

ARROWHEAD
BOOKS

First published November 1997
Copyright © RDO 1997

Published by
Arrowhead Books
Suite 201 - 37 Store Street
London WC1E 7BS.

ISBN 1 901674 43 6

CATALOGUE NO: AHB4100012

Printed and bound in the UK
by Bath Press

Purchase of this book in no way guarantees safety when the process of colonisation begins. To ensure that you are allowed to live as
labour or breeding stock we recommend that you purify your DNA. We strongly advise against starting up an underground resistance
movement as this will only antagonise your new masters and make things difficult for the rest of us.

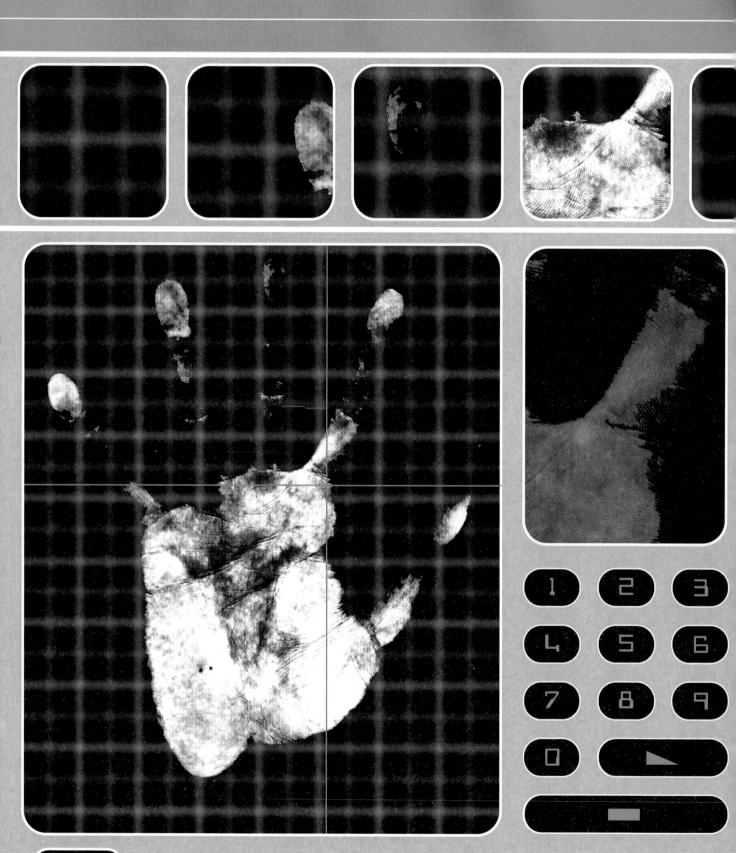

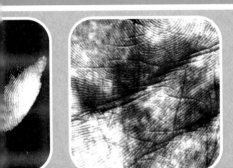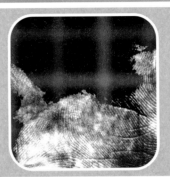

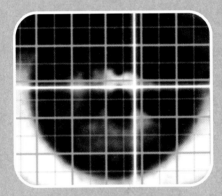

WARNING! YOU HAVE ENTERED A RESTRICTED AREA
UNAUTHORISED PERSONNEL FOUND BEYOND THIS POINT WILL BE SUBJECT TO
DEADLY FORCE WHEN CHALLENGED
PLEASE PRESENT YOUR ID CARD BEFORE PROCEEDING FURTHER

PLACE YOUR RIGHT PALM ON THE SCANNER FOR AUTHENTICATION

******PALM PRINT POSITIVE******

REMOVE ALL CONTACT LENSES, GLASSES OR OTHER EYE COVERINGS AND
LOOK DIRECTLY INTO THE LIGHT

******RETINAL SCAN POSITIVE******
PLEASE SPEAK YOUR NAME, RANK AND SERIAL NUMBER INTO THE MICRO-
PHONE

******VOICE PRINT POSITIVE******

ENTER PASSWORD
*******-****/***

WELCOME AGENT 9974-PMJ

******AREA UPDATE FOLLOWS******

THIS INFORMATION IS EYES ONLY AND REQUIRES SECURITY CLEARANCE LEVEL
Q-8 OR ABOVE. YOU ARE HEREBY AUTHORISED TO LIQUIDATE ANY PERSONS
GAINING ACCESS TO THIS REPORT TO MAINTAIN MISSION INTEGRITY

******

THIS GUIDE IS A COMPLETE UPDATE ON THE X-FILES SO FAR UNCOVERED BY
FBI AGENTS FOX MULDER AND DANA SCULLY, UP TO AND INCLUDING THE
'DEATH' OF AGENT MULDER. EXTRANEOUS EVIDENCE STILL EXISTS THAT
COULD COMPROMISE THE VIABILITY OF PLAUSIBLE DENIAL. USING THIS
INFORMATION YOU ARE EXPECTED TO FIND AND DESTROY SUCH EVIDENCE
UTILISING ALL MEANS AT YOUR DISPOSAL. YOUR SUCCESS IS VITAL TO THE
PROCESS OF COLONISATION WHICH IS SET TO COMMENCE IMMINENTLY.

******THIS IS NOT A COVERT OPERATION******

******USE OF DEADLY FORCE IS AUTHORISED******

******BACKGROUND INFORMATION FOLLOWS******

******DESTROY PRINTOUT AFTER ASSIMILATION******

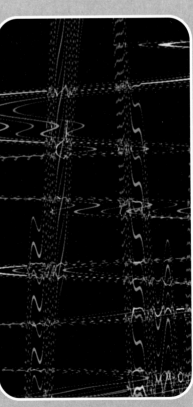

CONTENTS

ONE

X marks the spot

Chris Carter is the man behind the X-Files. It was his original idea and enthusiasm which gave us the first must-see television for the late nineties as the world gears itself up to go a little crazy come midnight on New Year's Eve, 1999. He started his career as editor of a surfing magazine called – you guessed it – *Surfing,* after graduating from Cal State Long Beach University with a degree in journalism. This proved to be an invaluable experience for him, as it enabled him to travel the world, surfing and writing. During this time he did a lot of pottery ("It's a Zen thing") and met his wife, Dori Pierson in 1983. He attributes his talents as a writer to a traumatic episode in his youth: "Alfred Hitchcock was locked up in a county jail by his dad, just for misbehaving. I was about eight years old and my dad did something so strange. I think he was crazy. I came home late one night past dinnertime. My dad took my plate out into the street, and he set it on a manhole cover, which is where I ate my dinner, with the cars going around me. That hasn't happened in an X-Files episode yet. But it may!"

Born and bred in the rarified atmosphere of Bellflower, California in a strict household, his early career as a writer and producer was with the Disney corporation, producing light-hearted comedies and family-orientated ideas for the company. He wrote a few screenplays which made it to the small screen, the unmemorable *B.R.A.T.Patrol* and *Meet The Munceys,* as well as writing and producing a pilot for Disney that went on to become *The Nanny*. From there he joined NBC and wrote many more pilots, none of which made a big enough impression on the executives to be picked up and it seemed that although a promising writer, Carter would find his success as a producer. As fate would have it, Peter Roth had just become head of television production at Fox, a man who had read some of Carters' work and wanted him on board, so Chris moved over to Fox where he was briefed to come up with story ideas.

A childhood favourite on television was a big influence in his life. A short-lived series called *Kolchak – The Night Stalker* followed the exploits of a detective as he fought against the forces of darkness amidst a background of government cover-ups and supernatural monsters. This stuck in his mind and when Chris was employed by the Fox Television Network as a story developer, he knew he wanted to make a story that captured those elements he loved so much about the old *Kolchak* stories – the paranoia, the sense of battling an unknowable foe – but put it in a nineties setting that would resonate with the pre-millenial tension that was sweeping the land. When he was watching the Letterman show he saw a guest whose job happened to be investigating the more tangible areas of the criminal occult scene – satanic covens, human sacrifices and the like – on behalf of the FBI. From then on he knew that his lead characters had to be FBI agents.

He wrote a pilot in his own time and felt that

the idea could work if somebody gave it the chance. Roth originally turned down the show but Carter had a lot more faith and pitched it again and again until the green light was given for a pilot to be filmed. The executives at Fox held out little hope for the show, seen as a rather cultish, underground thing compared to the show that was expected to be that years' big hit — *The Adventures Of Brisco County Junior*. Sorry, the adventures of who..? That's what the rest of the viewers thought and Brisco never made it past 1993.

The shooting script for the pilot called for two principal characters, the FBI agents — one a highly educated skeptic and the other an equally intelligent person who happens to be a devout believer in the paranormal. Carter knew pretty well who he wanted, but as is the way in the corporate system, the actors all had to audition for the parts in front of producers, directors and studio executives. For the male lead, Carter had had David Duchovny in mind from the start and due to his previous acting experience, encountered no problem convincing the powers that be that Duchovny was their man. For the female, rational lead, the casting decision was a lot harder. Many actresses were auditioned and the studio seemed set on vetoing every woman whose physical image didn't quite fit the image of the blonde bimbo fresh from sleazy flicks (ironically it was the male half of the duo who had a few embarrassing roles in his murky past). Carter knew it had to be Gillian Anderson from the moment he saw her walk in the room and fought

New directors would often fail to correctly handle David Duchovny's sensitive artistic temperament.

The production crew cruelly trick Mitch Pileggi into believing that horizontal stripes are slimming.

hard to get her for the part, although the studio retained the right to recast her if the pilot was not well received.

Carter had spent a lot of time researching the themes that would crop up within the X—Files world and although no great UFO or conspiracy enthusiast, now has a vast database of arcane lore to draw storylines from thanks to his internet fans, the infamous X-Philes. Whilst never having had a close encounter of either the extra-terrestrial or paranormal kind himself, he keeps an open mind on the subject – although his sympathies lie more with Scully than Mulder, even though her viewpoint has become untenable in the face of her numerous encounters with the inexplicable. Initially hostile to the project, the FBI has since relented and embraced the X-Files as a welcome positive look at their role in solving American criminal cases, letting the researchers poke around real offices to see what really goes on at the HQ. Research-wise, the series has been patchy at best, with some preposterous attempts at real science dragging the tenuous credibility of the show to rock bottom (*Soft Light*). Not that this really matters a jot to the audience, who either don't care about scientific inaccuracies or are happy to spend their time noting down mistakes before posting them on the Web.

More important to Carter was the sense of a coherent storyline that would hold the series together, keeping it on track with a sense of direction. There were to be two essential versions of the X-Files: the monster/paranormal episode and the Alien conspiracy plot, which initially received equal coverage but as the series has progressed it has become necessary to concentrate on the conspiracy plot. The two devices tend to work well in tandem, providing a balanced look at all that is unexplained in

"Yes, that's right – two livers and a bucket of slime to go, please."

was no doubt about it, the whole of the pilot depicted Fox as a barely-likable kook tilting at windmills, unwilling to come to terms with the facts....unbelievable, were it not for the start of the show when we actually saw for ourselves the aliens pop down and pick up an abductee. Curiously for a show that relied on suspense and a long story arc, it apparently showed us a substantial part of the truth straight away – the Aliens are out there and the government is covering it up. The ambiguities were only set up later, when we learn that it needn't necessarily be an Alien craft just because there are a few lights in the sky and mutated bodies rotting in freshly-dug graves.

There were numerous touches that set the episode apart from it's contemporaries. Due to the lower costs of shooting, production values were high and gave the show a polished, professional feel that lent itself to the thoroughness with which it treated it's material. It was the first show to feature the times of it's scenes right down to the very minute they took place in this fictional universe, giving the impression of following the official report. Unlike the regular police force, the FBI is supposed to operate all over the USA and so wildly different locations can be scripted (even if they are all shot in various parts of Canada). Carter lists amongst his inspirations both *The Twilight Zone*, which needs no explanation and top-rated British drama *Prime Suspect* for it's realism. He downplays the relevance of *Kolchak* as an inspiration for his mix of the tediously mundane world of a real criminal investigation with the wild fantasy of the conspiracy theorist (or alternatively, the absolutely true conspiracies with fictitious investigations, depending on whom you believe). The show walked a surefooted path through the jungle of nineties paranoia, coming down on neither side very firmly until the end of the first season.

The pilot went down well and the Fox Network took up the option to carry the series further. Not that many people knew it yet, but the X-Files had been discovered and were about to take over the world. Perhaps it is because the programme has that air of a hidden gem that it became such a success; there is undoubtedly the hand of an auteur at work no matter who did the writing or the directing for any one episode, which shows in an image devoid of corporate over-management. Or maybe the unseen authorities took steps to ensure that it was a success, because they want a prime-time show out there that confuses the public about the Alien presence – or is softening them up for a big admission that yes, the world is actually overrun by invaders from another planet.

modern society without providing the answers that we so obviously crave. The first show was by no means perfect and has dated somewhat since it's release, but it managed to set the tone for both of these core story threads, giving us the small-town America with undertones of conspiracies, cover-ups and psychic links. Carter had written it alone in his office, occasionally breaking off to play with the dog (it was that kind of an office) and the stories continue to be successfully driven by single-concept ideas and one or two writers, only lapsing into the committee-produced scripts that so many US shows have fallen foul of in it's latest season.

As this was a pilot with no history behind it, money was tight and financial reasons led the cast and crew to Vancouver, Canada, for shooting. The city is well up to the task of portraying any American urban landscape, but unlike film mecca Los Angeles there are no deserts or seafronts within easy reach, which helped give the series it's sharp look, away from the permasunshine of California. Written by Chris Carter and directed by Robert Mandel (who has yet to come back for another show) it set the tone for the rest of the series with it's themes of Alien abduction, Mulder's unshaking belief, Dana's challenging skepticism and government cover-ups.

The first of the pair we saw was Scully, in her long hair and glasses, being briefed on her next assignment by Skinner and some high-ranking associates. Told to assist Mulder in his work, she is also quietly asked to investigate the validity of his research into the paranormal by her superiors. The first we see of Mulder confirms her suspicions: a lonely figure in a broom cupboard of an office, covered in posters depicting UFO's and paranormal subjects. There

TWO

The Fox file

Our hero (sigh).

David Duchovny came into acting in a roundabout way. Born in 1960 in Manhattan, he was the son of Margaret, a teacher and Amram, a publicist. The family name is Eastern European in origin and has a religious slant to it — in Russian, it means 'spiritual' but in Czech it translates as 'Reverend'. On his Mother's side, the family is Scottish and David is a regular visitor to Aberdeen when he gets the chance. The Duchovny childhood was an uneventful one, punctuated only by the divorce of his parents when he was eleven. The family home was, spookily, opposite a graveyard. No X-Files episode has ever centered around a cemetery, which may or may not prove something.

Acting was never on the agenda for the young David, a keen academic student who studied at the elite Princeton College before going on to do a PhD at the prestigious Yale University. Once there, he caught the acting bug and starred in a number of university presentations before getting himself an agent. His first paycheque was $5,000 for a Lowenbrau beer commercial, but his career has hardly been smooth running since then. If anything, the X-Files was a step backward for Duchovny by the time he went to audition for the part.

His film career had gotten off to a promising start with *Julia Has Two Lovers,* a low budget

affair that brought him some recognition. In 1989 he found himself in a porn film, *New Year's Day*, which has since gained notoriety for his starring role. If you can find a copy for sale, expect to pay well over a hundred dollars for it. He has also starred in soft-core shtick *The Red Shoe Diaries*, a real triumph of crass anything-for-a-buck cinema over good taste if ever there was one. If you look closely at eighties throwback *Beethoven* you will find David being turned upside-down by the boisterous St. Bernard pooch, but don't watch it if you want to preserve some credibility for Mulder's character.

David Lynch's *Twin Peaks* gave him his first chance to play in a cult show, where Duchovny secured a part as a cross-dressing FBI agent helping Kyle Maclachan's Agent Cooper in his inquiries. Probably his best-known role outside of the X-Files was in the serial-killer flick *Kalifornia*. Playing a writer touring the US, researching a book on America's most gruesome killings, he and his girlfriend pick up a pair of travelling partners who begin putting some new points on the murder map of the USA. The film was not bad by any standards, but was up against stiff competition in the form of Oliver Stone's more controversial murder-marathon *Natural Born Killers* and failed to set the box-office alight. The strong cast went on to do

much better things – Brad Pitt played the psychopathic redneck and is now the world's heartthrob, Juliette Lewis is never short of work and Michelle Forbes, playing opposite Duchovny, went on to play Ensign Ro, the Bajoran officer in *Star Trek: The Next Generation* and now has a regular role in police drama *Homicide: Life On The Street*.

Because of his extensive previous experience as an actor, he was the natural choice for the part of Fox Mulder when the auditions came and the decision had to be made between him and another actor. There are also claims he impressed the executives with his wit and charm, though why

Look Scully, those are our fans.

Fox Mulder: Great hair.
Great suit. Crap tie.

they then gave him the pilot show where he displayed neither is anyone's guess. Duchovny's easy-going nature on set is legendary, as is his appetite for romantic liaisons off-set. He is reputed to have checked in at one point to a Hollywood "sex addiction" clinic but this is almost certainly one of the press' more extravagant versions of the truth. Duchovny has admitted being on the wayward side where it comes to women and has been linked not only with Gillian Anderson in the newspapers but with various starlets, including Winona Ryder at one time. During the filming of the X-Files, he split up with his long-time lover Perry Reeves (whom he met while choosing a suit) but is now happily married to his new love after she forced him to tie the knot or finish with her. The lucky lady was Tea Leone, a pretty young thing who can currently be seen on the small screen in her sit-com series *The Naked Truth,* where she stars as a tabloid hack. The one thing he has remained faithful to all these years is his dog Blue, a border collie/terrier cross which gets it's atmospheric name from the Bob Dylan song *Tangled*

clothes on ("It took me ages to finish!" he complained). He is reputed to have enlivened a promotional photo-shoot by stripping off and covering his top secret information with a teapot. He is a basketball freak and never misses a game of his hometown team. His Scottish mother likes to watch his work, but she will always ask him if he is to appear naked or die in his next project – if the answer is yes to either question, she refuses to watch!

He has recently finished a feature *Playing God,* but rumours have it that much to his annoyance, the film will be destined for delays and a straight-to-video release. He is curiously reluctant to talk about his work on the X-Files as he values his privacy above all else (this from the man who has bared all to the cameras on numerous occasions and thinks nothing of countless publicity shots, walking around topless or with his shirt hanging off in the series...I could go on). When he is coerced to

Up In Blue and his father (Blue's father, not David's) has appeared in the first series of the show.

Duchovny is a curious fellow. On the one hand, there is the serious intellect who studied for a PhD at Yale and could have gone on to become a professor or lecturer. On the flip side, we have wisecracking Duchovny the actor, whose sense of humour and way with the ladies suggests a different person altogether. He is inundated with marriage proposals every week from besotted women around the globe and once received a jigsaw puzzle a female fan had sent in, which made up a picture of her with no

speak on things X, he toes the party line about the show being a reflection of modern mythology, how it plays upon our preconceptions about the unknown, why the success only breeds more paranoia and more material for the show...this is not the voice of the man who has recently taken such an interest in the storylines of the programme.

Duchovny has expressed an interest in taking a more active role in the plot of the show, taking credit for some story ideas in seasons two and three. His first, in association with Chris Carter, was *Colony,* which introduced the shape-shifting bounty-hunter and the clones of

Mulder's sister, advancing the conspiracy plot. He and Carter were also responsible for the original story of season two cliffhanger *Anasazi,* and continues his ideas along the Alien conspiracy with *Talitha Cumi* and it's concluding part *Herrenvolk.* The only other episode Duchovny claims credit for is *Avatar,* which sees Assistant Director Skinner in a spot of bother with his love life and shies away from the larger story arc. Why he should want to do this when he already has a glittering career behind and in front of him, enough money to retire today (thanks to a wage estimated to start from $100,000 a show) is a mystery. Perhaps he wants, like most actors, to have something to fall back on when he is old and grey and no longer flavour of the month.

As an actor, he has stated that the X-Files is, like a permanent role in a popular soap or series like *Star Trek,* something that made him famous and with which he will always be associated. To him though, it's just another job in a career that has spanned roles in slapstick comedy, soft-porn and mass-market advertisements and will not be the last role he will ever play. Apart from the forthcoming X-Files film, he sees his future in movies and features rather than television productions. Rumours of his leaving the X-Files before or after the imminent fifth season abound, but with Chris Carter saying that his involvement with the series will end after the fifth season and the completion of the film, it is clear that the future for X-Files fans is not going to be an eternity of fresh episodes.

The Mulder household hides a multitude of sins. What other family could claim to comprise of an ex-conspirator (William Mulder), a Ufologist and paranormal investigator (Fox), an alien abductee (Samantha) and an amnesiac for a mother (see *Talitha Cumi*)? It's no wonder that Fox turned out to be a manic obsessive. Born on the 13th October 1961 (which makes him a Libra, constantly seeking balance in his life), the name Fox came not from some form of undisguised sycophancy on the part of Carter towards his employers, but was from a child Chris had once known in school whose unusual first name deserved national attention. His lifelong quest to find out the truth behind

his sister's abduction began when Samantha Mulder was taken from her room when she was eight years old and Fox was twelve. This is held as a self-evident truth of the series (although there have been attempts to undermine his faith – see *Little Green Men* and *Paper Hearts*) which fuels Mulder's enormous drive to uncover the truth, no matter what the cost.

Mulder's career seems to have been in part inspired by the academic path followed by Duchovny. Fox has studied psychology at Oxford

A hairspray failure can ruin a good photoshoot.

(a feature in his life that popped up when he met an old flame in *Fire*) and chose to join the FBI as a means of using it's resources to further his own investigations. This seems to have been to no avail however, as he admits in the pilot episode that an unknown organisation is blocking his attempts to progress any further. In 1988 he wrote a paper on "Serial Killers And The Occult" which helped catch a serial killer named Monty Props and he is widely regarded as a leading expert in violent crime and a gifted analyst of the criminal mind.

He studied at the Investigative Support Unit at Quantico with Bill Patterson, a behavioural sciences guru who later got a little close to his subject and began a double life as a serial killer (*Grotesque*) before being apprehended by his old pupil. Mulder's rise as an FBI agent seems to have been on the fast track to high places (just as Scully's was before she became involved with him) until he slipped into the darker alleyways of the paranormal and the disreputable side of FBI investigations, earning him the "Spooky" title. The X-Files do actually exist in the catacombs of certain places in the various departments of government investigators the world over, but whether or not they are entered with the vigour and regularity given to them by Mulder and Scully is adding more than a little gloss to the mundane reality (Duchovny once asked a real FBI agent what he could do to make the role more true to life. Without hesitation, he replied "more paperwork"). Unsolved cases in real life that involve occult connections are just not treated with the respect and reverence that Mulder gives them, but go along with all the other cases awaiting conclusion in an unclosed file (so perhaps the show should have been called the U-Files).

Fox's father, Bill Mulder, has now been revealed as a member of the secret group which has known about the existence and presence on Earth of the Aliens (firstly in *Colony* and *End Game*) but did not live to tell his son the whole story as he was shot by Alex Krycek in season two finale *Anasazi*. Along with the Cigarette Smoking Man (CSM) and Deep Throat, Bill was seen in a photograph linking him to war criminal Victor Klemper (*Paper Clip*) who formed a group that started the nefarious experiments on Human and possibly Alien subjects. It is implicitly stated that Bill had a moral problem with what he was getting himself into that kept him from

Who's that handsome guy over there? Why, me of course!

being a full part of the conspiracy, so his relationship with CSM is probably the only reason that Mulder is still alive. The troubles between Fox's parents seem to stem from the time when the Mulders used to go on holiday to a country house where the CSM and Deep Throat came along. There are hints that CSM may have enjoyed a closer relationship with Mrs Mulder than Bill would have liked and even that he may be Fox's father (*Talitha Cumi* and *Musings Of a Cigarette Smoking Man* where CSM carries a picture of her

Dialling for pizza in the X-Files is a hazardous business

and baby Fox).

The series has seen Mulder through more than his fair share of life-changing experiences. The pilot portrayed him as a rather cold, passion-less observer of the facts, only getting involved personally when the parallels with his sister were introduced, as the series doesn't seem to know whether or not Fox is looking for some answers just for himself or to alert the public at large. He is ready at a moments' notice to hightail it out of town and go off on a life-risking venture (*Fallen Angel*), jeopar-dising life and limb to obtain some fragment of proof and in doing so, tends to endanger the lives of all his nearest and dearest. Fox Mulder is an X-File himself in this way – wherever he goes, people end up dying or severely changed in some way. Think about it – would you want to join him as he goes off to another deserted location, facing unknown and typically messily lethal foes? His partner and possibly the only person he trusts in the world has been shot at, abducted, imprisoned, tied up, kidnapped, lost close family members and is now dying of can-cer. His boss was beaten up and almost got put away for murder (*Avatar*). His dad got shot. Every conspiracy member brave enough to even

speak to him has been bumped off. His old teacher became a serial killer. Potential girl-friends have been burned to death (3). Let's face it, Mulder's a jinx.

With a past record like that, it's no wonder he has developed into a paranoid, gun-toting guy, susceptible to any claim that gives him the slightest glimmer of hope that he will be reunited with his long-lost sibling or that he will learn the truths hidden from him by the conspiracy. In *The Field Where I Died* he dis-plays a worrying tendency to grasp at straws, looking for some way to belong somewhere even if it means resorting to new-age psychobabble and past-life 'regression therapy' (even the staunchest believer must side with Scully at this point, as all the principle characters in the series seem to make an appearance in a con-centration camp, despite the fact that CSM would have been alive and just out of nappies at the time of World War II).

It's not just deranged women who claim to be former lovers that can sway his judgment. Serial killers, not normally noted for their rational outlook on life, will almost always have, or claim to have, some sort of psychic powers

A Fox in a Tux is worth two in the bush. Probably.

(*Pusher, Paper Hearts*) and their offer to share their gifts with you must be very tempting (*Beyond The Sea*). When they have had proven paranormal powers, they have only been of the destructive, physical variety (*The Walk, Fire*) rather than the subtle arts of precognition (*Clyde Bruckman's Final Repose*) or telepathy (*Oubliette*). Mulder's willing suspension of disbelief has weakened the character somewhat because he used to be such a good skeptic, believing only what he could prove with his own eyes and ears. But now, after seeing so much and having gone through so many ordeals, it is probably only fair to assume that any new lead will be true. Carter has said that his original idea for the slant of the series would be that the agents would face a 50/50 mix of real psychics and Aliens with an equal number of hoaxers and charlatans, yet so far the only real faker we have seen is the Stupendous Yappi (from *Clyde Bruckman's...* and an obvious cipher for Uri Geller), coupled with some "monsters" which have turned out to be rather sorry examples of Humanity gone bad (*The Jersey Devil, Home*). Somewhere along the line, Carter's vision of an evenly-balanced view has gone out the window and the series has developed into a real-life free zone.

For poor old Fox, this has led to a crisis of faith but not for the usual reasons. While he has been given some occasional reason to doubt his convictions, he has now surely uncovered enough to convince either himself or any other skeptic (including Scully) that everything he ever believed in was true. What on Earth makes him get up in the morning? Whatever he discovers about the conspiracy now will only be further embellishment on what he already knows, so the only thing he could possibly want is his sister back. There may be some hope for this that drives him on as the alien bounty-hunter told him she was still alive (*End Game*) and clones of her are abundant in America (*Colony, Herrenvolk*). Another driving force could be his desire to tell the public about the conspiracy and of the sheer weirdness that is out there, but he could do this at any time by simply taking a news crew along on one of his jaunts to the lesser-known villages of the US to film a new X-File with him. When Deep Throat called him up to see the crash site in *Fallen Angel* or when he set off to the jungle SETI centre in *Little Green Men* all he had to do was alert the reporters of the worlds' news gatherers and let them helicopter him in and out (if nothing else, it would have at least saved him from a bumpy ride along a dirt road).

He would never do anything like that of course, because the series cannot (and should not) cater to real concerns. The pilot show was said to have been based on real-life accounts, yet this was barley a nod of acknowledgment towards the UFO abduction stories that have been around for some time. If there is anything real-life about the series it is the identity of Fox, a lonely man driven to extreme behaviour by the extraordinary sights he has witnessed while searching for a lost childhood. Is it any wonder he is a keen consumer of pornography and cannot hold down a stable relationship, sleeps on his couch with the TV on and works in a tiny office in self-imposed exile? This is not the behaviour of a man who believes anymore and like the ill-fated X and all his fellow conspirators, is destined to be destroyed by the secrets they all hold so dear.

You lookin' at me, punk?

The life of Gillian Anderson could easily be a good story on it's own before the chance to be in the X-Files came up. Born and bred in Crouch End, London, Anderson grew up with a British accent and had an uneventful early childhood in the suburbs. Her parents were well off and provided a comfortable home for Gillian. It was when they relocated to the USA that her so-called wild-child years began, in part as a rebellion for taking her away from the culture she had grown up in (it wasn't all bad — at least she could provide a decent English accent for *Fire* even if she should have reminded the producers that their version of England was a hundred years out of date). It was in America that Anderson took to the punk lifestyle and grew her hair into brightly-coloured spikes, rejected all authority, skipped school and shacked up with a twenty-four year-old man while still fourteen.

That she has now found fame as a paragon of straight-laced office-girl desirability is one of life's little ironies and proof that Anderson is a much bet-

ter actress than anyone gives her credit for. Unlike Duchovny, she always has been a career actress and after graduating from the Grand Rapids public school, Michigan, she knew that the theatre was going to be the only place where she could find any results in her life and auditioned for a place in Chicago's Goodman Theatre School, a subsidiary of the DePaul University (which, to all non-American trivia buffs out there, is a big deal within the acting community). Once set up inside the city of *ER* and *Chicago Hope* she couldn't help but succeed and got parts in various stage plays off Broadway, earning herself a Theatre World Award for her role in the play *Absent Friends*. Her screen roles were less exalted, including feature film *The Turning* and a part in Fox TV's *Class Of '96*, which brought her to the attention of Chris Carter. It was he who championed the part of Scully for Anderson, having reportedly decided on her for the role as soon as she entered the room.

It's now common knowledge that Gillian was not the studio's first choice, owing to her general lack of top-heavy blondness (however, prurient viewers may note her augmented screen presence whilst hospitalised in *One Breath* – apparently they enlarge after giving birth, but this is ridiculous). Carter all but staked his reputation on Anderson and proved himself spectacularly right, changing the world's perception of sophisticated ginger people on television despite Chris Evans' valiant attempts to the contrary. Anderson is now accepted as one of the world's most beautiful women, and has topped the polls of the glossies in every country

Following FBI rules of etiquette, contraband drugs should always be sniffed in the RIGHT hand with the little finger extended.

My extensive work on this case enables me to deduce that this man is dead.

where the X-Files is aired. Why a former punk queen playing an often rather dowdy criminal investigator should enjoy such universal appeal is hard to quantify. Is it her on-screen chemistry with Duchovny? Her fetching displays of authority and meticulously executed autopsies? It's just one of those things that has made the series such a success and if the studio knew what it was, they wouldn't bother with random auditions to get the actors they wanted.

Anderson laughs off the attention, claiming not to be bothered by her position as a sex-godess. Her new-found star status may get her a table at any restaurant in town, but her turbulent personal life has inevitably come under the microscope of the celebrity-watchers. That she has never been out with Duchovny socially is a source of great bitterness and resentment for the press, who ignored this little fact and, during the early days of the first rush of popularity, constantly claimed that the pair were closer than they would admit. Now that she and David have had a chance

to speak for themselves, the sad truth has come out that their relationship in real life has stayed as it was during the first series – they work together amiably but do not socialise afterwards. Duchovny is now a happily married man and Gillian has split up with ex-hubby Clyde Klotz, an X-Files designer and father of her child Piper (after whom the two-parter *Piper Maru* was named). Reports tell that Klotz was using his skills to carve a four-poster bed for the happy couple, but what became of it, post-separation, is unknown. Her latest love affair to hit the headlines was said to be with actor Adrian Hughes, whom she met on-set (he was playing one of the deformed yokels in *Home*, so the guy must have one hell of a personality to attract Gillian whilst wearing monster make-up). Neither have confirmed or denied the rumours, but since Hughes was arrested in Canada for five counts of indecent assault in January '97, Anderson has taken steps to distance herself from him.

Gillian now has property in Vancouver and LA and has been seen around London once again (would you believe crowdsurfing at a Camden nightspot?), enjoying her new free'n'single lifestyle. It would seem she now has the world at her feet. Co-star of a major TV show, an international beauty, rich beyond the dreams of avarice...except that she is paid substantially less than Duchovny for her part in the X-Files. Acting is still one of the last bastions of unequal male/female pay rates, with top

male stars earning millions more than their lady compadres. Roseanne Barr is to date the only leading lady to come close to the power and control which the men expect as their due, like Bill Cosby who earned an unfathomably vast $60m a season during the last Cosby Show years and went on to buy the studio! Although Duchovny and Anderson do not quite compare to this, the difference between the two is still marked. "I'm more than adequately compensated," she states curtly. Whether or not she takes an interest in the story of the show like David is a mystery, but knowing that your on-screen partner gets more money and a say in the scripts and story arc cannot be a big morale booster.

What Gillian Anderson does have the franchise on is the last word in working-girl chic, from her finely sculpted hair and porcelain features to the toes of her Teflon shoes (are they ever dirty?). Check how many different suits she wears over the course of the show – it's no wonder the US government has crime problems when it's law enforcers must be spending all of their time shop-

ping for clothes. For those of us not blessed with a workwear allowance that exceeds the minimum wage, we must be content with the knowledge that Anderson deserves every last penny. As her character has evolved from skeptical scientist to abductee and terminally-ill cancer sufferer, Anderson has never let us doubt her talent as an actress and has shown a depth of feeling that belies her tender age (she read for the pilot when only twenty-five). Now the only demanding choice she faces when getting out of bed is whether or not to stay in the series that has treated her so kindly for the past four years and commit herself to another season, which may be her last. Unlike Duchovny, she has lots of theatre experience to fall back on and she is not overtly seeking a new life as a movie star like David is.

was revealed he and Dana had touching little nicknames for each other (he was Ahab, a rather obvious naval reference from Herman Melville's *Moby Dick*. She was Starbuck, a less well-known Moby Dick name but also the lead in *Battlestar Galactica*, a popular Sci-fi series from the stable of Chris Carter's eighties equivalent, Glen A. Larson)

At the time of the pilot, Agent Scully had already been with the FBI for two years.

She started life out training to be a doctor but left to join the Feds, much to the disapproval of her parents. A keen intellect, she did a degree at the teaching academy in physics while lecturing at Quantico (where Mulder studied and met the soon-to-be-unhinged Bill Patterson). Her graduation thesis was the intriguingly titled "Einstein's Twin Paradox: A New Interpretation", but considering the paradox is an accepted fact of science (the one where the twin goes off to space at close to light speed and returns to find his identical brother is now older than he is), one can only wonder what mark she got. She drinks coffee with cream and no sugar (*E.B.E.*).

Her family life is, for the most part, much more settled than Mulder's. Outside of her immediate family she has a little godson (Trent, son of her friend Ellen – *The Jersey Devil*) and has been known to go out on dates. Her father, a Navy Captain, met his maker in first season tear-jerker *Beyond The Sea*, where it

which surfaced again in *One Breath* and *Quagmire*. It was his supernatural appearance to her that led her to soften her views on the paranormal, coupled with the relentless way with which the unnamed government factions confound her and Mulder's attempts to get to the answers.

If there is one thing fans of the Files get annoyed at, it is the regularity with which Scully manages to arrive two seconds too late to see any first-hand evidence. Not content with this, she feels compelled (at least in the first two seasons) to offer her own explanation of that week's events in scientific detail. Time after time, she refuses to believe Mulder's version and comes up with her own piece of cold rationalisation. Little Kevins' drawings in *Conduit*? A statistical aberration. The UFO's in *Deep Throat*? Lasers bouncing off the clouds. Duane Barry's metal fragments implanted in his head? From Vietnam. Like the Doubting Thomas she is, it has taken nothing less than the equivalent of Jesus popping in and showing her his wounds before she has shown any faith

(*Wetwired* took her over the edge of the paranoid event horizon and she has never been the same since). It was when her somewhat irritating new-age sister got shot in season three opener *The Blessing Way* that the reality of the situation she was in really hit her. Thus the Human conspiracy, which put the computer chip in the back of her neck, is a known enemy but even after fighting off such horrors as Eugene Tooms, the sewer full of cats in *Teso Dos Bichos* and the impossible psychic version of trading places in *Oubliette*, she cannot bring herself to confirm Mulder's more out-there theories on the paranormal. She is yet to explain who or what threw her about the room at the end of *The Calusari*, though.

Unlike Mulder, who had faith from the start, she has had belief thrust upon her by events. After seeing the files and the childlike Mutants/Aliens in *Paperclip*, no-one could say there isn't something slightly fishy going on. The Scully we see as season four progresses is a very different one to the hesitant Dana, rushing over to Fox when she finds a mark on the back of her neck in the pilot episode (which turned out to be a sinister premonition of things to come). What happened to the plucky little tomboy who shot a grass snake to death with her brothers? Like Mulder, she has now seen too much to return to anything resembling a normal life. Not that she doesn't try — her valiant attempts to keep scientific curiosity at the forefront of their investigations are a real triumph of hope over experience. As is any attempt on her part to get back into the social scene. Unlike Mulder, old acquaintances just don't seem to be part of the equation for Scully. The only time we see her have any sort of on-screen relationship is in the fourth season and only then as an extreme reaction to her status as a cancer victim. In *Never Again* she throws caution to the

wind and dates *Space: Above And Beyond* refugee Rodney Rowland, getting herself a tattoo in the process (it is of an Uroborus — the snake eating it's own tail, a symbol of eternity — that is also in the titles of Carter's new series, *Millennium*) and otherwise acting very un-Scullylike. The events leading up to her encounter with incurable illness were started in season two double-parter *Duane Barry* and *Ascension*, where they encountered a real abductee driven to madness by his experiences, the Duane of the title. Brilliantly played by Steve Railsback, who gave Duane his nervy yet slightly apologetic presence, it was also a badly-kept secret that Anderson was by this stage heavily pregnant with Clyde Klotz' baby, which explained Scully's absence from the series during the next two episodes and her mysterious preference for standing behind large desks and wearing shapeless baggy lab-coats.

After her return following the traitorous Krycek's ignominious exit, it took more than a year for the true implications to surface, when season three two-parter *Nisei* and *731* yielded a few more nuggets of conspiracy information. Scully chances upon a group of women who have also experienced an abduction scenario. Following their lead, she finds and has removed some sort of computer chip. Her exchange with the FBI electronics expert betrays a quiet surprise to learn that it is of Earthly origin ("You mean it's man-made?" — "What else would it be?") and shatters the beliefs of many of the viewers to discover that maybe the Aliens are not the abductors. Her relief is short-lived, as it transpires that all the women who have gone through these experiments are doomed to a long, drawn-out death due to some form of inoperable cancer.

This possible future for Scully is tactfully ignored for the rest of the third season as she and Mulder battle more immediately lethal foes in the form of demonically empowered teenagers (*Syzygy*) and deadly Alien slime (*Piper Maru*), while the time bomb inside her ticks away. We have to wait until the fourth season is well under way before the issue of Scully's mortality is addressed properly, first in weirdo mutant-land with *Leonard Betts*, who is himself a living, sentient cancerous tumour. His need to feed off the cancer cells of normal humans coupled with his ability to sniff out the unfortunate sufferers leads him eventually to Scully, who later wakes up to find blood on her pillow, confirming the diagnosis. The sentimental *Memento Mori* follows swiftly, where Dana tells Fox that she is terminally ill, prompting him to turn to CSM for help. The group of women from *Nisei* have all died off except for one severely ill woman who tells Scully of a possible new treatment, which has so far proven ineffective.

Since then, rumours have flown that Scully is set to leave the series, either for Gillian Anderson to pursue other avenues (she is currently working on a non-X feature) or because the stories about her demanding equal wages are true. The latter is less likely at present because she and Duchovny have reportedly received $5m each for their roles in the forthcoming X-Files film (speculation that they were to be replaced by Richard Gere and Jodie Foster in the film has proven groundless). It is true that she and David are not exactly bosom buddies off the set, but there is currently no cause for concern that Gillian will be leaving the series before the end of the fifth season. If you have any faith in the long-term story arc, then bear in mind the charming Clyde Bruckman's enigmatic words to Dana when she speaks to him.

"Okay, how do I die?" (cute knowing smile) "You don't". Is she destined to end up in some sort of Alien-generated null space? To become truly immortal through the experiments? To live on forever as a series of clones, like Mulder's sister? We should treat Clyde's predictions with a pinch of salt however, as he chose his own method of death, cheating the predictions that had so far proven so horrifyingly true.

At the moment, Dana stands alone as a pillar of fortitude by Mulder as he grows increasingly unstable and at the same time, closer to the truth. If Chris Carter holds true to his word and the fifth series is the last to feature his involvement, it would be like Gene Roddenberry leaving *Star Trek* (some might say this is no bad thing having seen the difference between *ST: TNG* before and after Roddenberry's help). As much as we would all like to think otherwise, Duchovny and Anderson have real lives which don't revolve around the X-Files and in order to have careers outside of their time with Carter, a sixth series and beyond without it's main creator may prove to be one step too far for the credibility of the show. Whatever happens, it is a very brave move to make a lead role in a prime-time TV show a terminally-ill cancer sufferer, even if she does have a definite get-out-of-jail-free card in the form of rebel Alien Jeremiah Smith, who along with all other shapeshifters possesses the ability to cure humans of all ills (*Talitha Cumi, Herrenvolk*).

Coming from a religious family, it is not surprising that the only piece of jewellery she allows herself to wear is a gold necklace with a cross. First noticed in *Deep Throat*, it becomes relevant when it is all that Mulder can find of her when she is abducted in *Ascension* and Dana's mother, Margaret, tells Fox

that it was given to her when she was fifteen and that he should keep it. Mulder reacts in a very strange manner after Scully's disappearance, in a much more extreme way than one would expect from a normal working partnership. In fact, every episode after the first season contains little telling gestures between the pair that reveal a closer relationship than might otherwise be expected - a brush of the hair here, a casual arm around the shoulder when a handshake would suffice - check out Mulder wiping away the tomato sauce from Scully's face in *Red Museum* - is that the sign of an intimate relationship or what? It was directed by Win Phelps, who never returned to the series after that. Punishment for letting them get too close? It didn't do the show any harm, as the sexual tension between Fox and Dana is widely regarded as being the main source of entertainment from the show next to it's paranormal themes. Anderson has been quoted as saying that it would be all right for the on-screen agents to show a more physical side to their relationship, but only if it was the last episode - "If it's the end, we're allowed to". It's true that like the lamentable descent of *Moonlighting* into madness, for the two leads to share a duvet is suicide. We came close in *Small Potatoes,* where a Mulder-lookalike came within micrometers of planting a smacker on Scully's lips, but was saved at the last moment by a contrived plotline. Considering that the core audience demographic is the under-35 male, the producers have at least given plenty of scope for Dana to play the woman-in-peril while some psychopath slobbers over her (*Squeeze, Ascension, Irresistible, Leonard Betts*). Erm, thanks. As if there aren't enough posters of the scantily-clad Ms Anderson available. Whenever she feels that she's just a sex object, Gillian can just curl up with her Emmy award for Best Female Actor in a Dramatic Series and count her money while beating back ardent suitors with a stick. Tough life.

FOUR

The X men

Skinner keeps calm while desparately trying to fend off the deadly fingernail-eating shirt monster.

And woman. Mulder and Scully do most of the work, but there are times when the burden of being the sole FBI agents investigating the X-Files becomes too much and help is needed. For Fox and Dana, this comes in the form of anonymous tip-offs from shady types who favour the seventies-detective raincoat look. Who are these people? And why do they risk their lives to give Mulder information that is misleading, unclear or even dangerously wrong?

There aren't that many people on Mulder and Scully's side. Of those that are, they are none too quick to divulge the secrets that Fox yearns for so keenly. The most vigorous supporter of their search has so far been Assistant Director Skinner, played by veteran actor Mitch Pileggi (who has drawn a sizable pool of admirers, including a Website by adoring female fans). His first appearance in *Tooms* came at a time when the daring duo had just finished off one of the series most enduring monsters, the stretchy-limbed Eugene where he appeared along with CSM, who had authority over the FBI number two — which should have been warning enough for Mulder that his productive days as a harmless investigative agent into the otherworldly invaders were numbered (CSM's first words were "Of course I do", when asked if he believed Mulder's and Scully's report on Tooms). The working relationship between CSM and Skinner has been strained at best, with Skinner coming off worse almost every time. In the course of following his duty and helping out Mulder when he can, Walter has been shot, beaten up, framed and defiantly smoked at (by CSM, who else, in *One Breath* – although Skinner curiously has an ashtray in his non-smoking office), all of which are certainly in breach of FBI employee regulations.

Skinner's image is of a man who has worked his way up to a top job from the bottom rung of the ladder. He served in Vietnam, where he underwent some harrowing experiences as well as an out-of-body episode which has left him more sympathetic to Mulder's theories than another boss might be. The character of Walter S. Skinner has progressed since his first appearance and developed some very fetching shades of grey to his persona, displaying a man trapped by the position he is in. He has all the privileges of his position but the compromises he is forced to take by the forces of the dark side show what is essentially a thoroughly decent man fighting a losing battle with his inner demons. He manages to support his proteges well though, and displays a curious courage throughout the series. He risks his job and probably his life by giving Mulder CSM's address, protects the Navajo-encoded information on the experiments (*The Blessing Way*) and is steely-nerved enough to face a damn good thrashing from X (*End Game*) to safeguard Fox. Who could ask for more from their Assistant Director?

Well, you could ask him to take a bullet, because that too is what Skinner has suffered in the course of duty, in *Piper Maru* where he also fought to keep open the investigation into Melissa Scully's death. Poor old Skinner, he's even had a rough old time just when he needed his privacy in *Avatar*, being framed for killing a prostitute and seeing strange ghostly women that hark back to his days

in Vietnam. Visiting an escort agency does nothing for his marriage, which by this time is understandably entering a rough phase due to an assassination attempt on him and his wife, Sharon, who now lies comatose thanks to being run off the road by a conspiracy agent. Meeting her in her hospital bed, he decides not to go ahead with divorce proceedings (he's all heart). Their wedding ring is inscribed with the uncharacteristically gooey "Love Forever, Sharon".

The S stands for Sergei.

The informant know only as Deep Throat had a major influence over the first series. Some sort of highly influential member of the conspiracy and the government, he is a cautious operator who started Mulder off on his search for the proof of extra-terrestrials with a telephone call to warn him away from the UFO's at Ellens Air Base (*Deep Throat*). He made sporadic appearances throughout the first season, his most important and revealing coming in *E.B.E.*, where most of the truth about the Aliens is explained to the audience. Here we learn that there is an international conspiracy and that Deep Throat, who was in the CIA, is a member of it. He tells Fox that after the Roswell incident in 1947, there was a convention attended by the USA, the then-USSR, Britain, Germany, China and France on the subject of Aliens. It was decided that whenever a creature was found on the planet, the country holding it would be responsible for it's extermination. Deep Throat is one of three men on Earth to have done so (the truck driver, actually Frank Druce, a Black Beret, is another – the third man is yet to be revealed). It was found after the Marines shot down a UFO flying over Hanoi during the Vietnam conflict and it's innocent, blank expression as he shot it was the catalyst for his change of heart and is why he tried to help Mulder – to assuage his guilt in some way.

He pays the ultimate price for his sins in *The Erlenmyer Flask*, shot by the crew-cut man for indiscretion. His final words on this side of the spirit divide as he dies in Scully's arms (aww!) are "Trust no one" (what else), implying that he was killed on the orders of a former friend. This was probably CSM, who knew Deep Throat along with Bill Mulder since they were young men. It could have also been X, who had to do it in order to safeguard his position within the conspiracy. Both X and Bill Mulder were to meet similarly violent deaths in future episodes.

The part of Deep Throat is played by Jerry Hardin, an actor of many years and one who has through no fault of his own become associated with science fiction roles. As a distinguished actor who studied in Britain's prestigious Royal Academy of Dramatic Art on a scholarship, he could have made a very good living on the stage on both sides of the Atlantic but drifted into television and films with parts in *Cujo, Reds, The Firm* and even came away from *Big Trouble In Little China* with his dignity intact. His television credits include such leading lights as *The New Adventures Of Superman, Quantum Leap, Star Trek: The Next Generation* and *Voyager*, but it is his part in the X-Files that has given him the exposure that all actors crave. Of his unexpected popularity, he merely states that he is pleased at the reaction the fans gave him for what was essentially, a few lines out of a whole season plus some nether-world mumbo-jumbo as a ghost in *The Blessing Way*. Chris Carter once said to him that no one really dies on the X-Files, so maybe there will be a comeback for the troubled man to right past wrongs. For the moment, he's happy to pick up the cheque for a half-day's work whenever a shapeshifter needs to use his face (*Talitha Cumi*).

Taking over his role in the fight was X, played by Steven Williams. He introduced himself by leading Mulder to the Vietnam Veterans in *Sleepless*, after a couple of anonymous 'phone calls in *The Host*, but his is a very different attitude and he makes it clear that he has no intention of making the sacrifice that Deep Throat made, so DT must have known that death was the only result of his actions. X proved a much more practical insider than Deep Throat ever was, preferring the harsh rule of gun law to the subtle art

of diplomacy. This tactic comes to a head in *731* where he saves Mulder's life by blowing away an NSA agent and carrying the unconscious Fox to safety. He is never above a nice bit of violence, particularly if it involves beating up someone who has no chance of winning (Skinner in *End Game* and some hapless lackey in *One Breath*). From the moment he starts helping Fox though, he must surely know his days are numbered. Sure enough, he meets a grisly end at the beginning of the fourth season, caught by a conspiracy trap to test his loyalty (one suspects there is no provision for a pension plan for conspiracy members). Shot to death, in true Hollywood tradition he manages to scrawl a message in blood: SRSG, the Special Representative to the Secretary General (a very sloppy killing on behalf of the Men In Black, who usually make sure their target is stone dead before leaving the scene).

This new lead takes our protagonists to Marita Covarrubias, the Special representative's assistant. She provides Mulder with proof of yet more Samantha clones while outwardly denying any knowledge of the conspiracy and goes on to help Mulder with his investigations into the colour-draining Samuel Aboah (*Talk*) and helps with his search for the truth on the Alien slime in *Tunguska*, amongst other appearances in season 4. Marita and her boss prove the most effective state-helpers, much more so than Senator Richard Matheson, who was only able to point Fox at Arecibo, light the blue touch paper and let go. The group who have provided the most value for money has so far been the Lone Gunmen, an "extreme government watchdog" accord-

ing to Mulder (*E.B.E*). A self-confessed group of Net-pickers ("We're all hopping on the Internet to nitpick the scientific inaccuracies of Earth 2" – *One Breath*), they take their name from the newsletter they edit, which contains all manner of information on the covert actions of the state. Between the triumvirate of Frohike, Langley and Byers, the Gunmen possess an encyclopaedic knowledge of everything Fox could ever want to know, from radioactive insects (*Blood*) to Japanese shipping routes (*Nisei*) and beyond. Reputedly included as a tribute to the real-life Net-heads who helped make the programme what it is, there is some truth in the idea that the Gunmen are inspired in part by reality – the X-Files, due to the nature of the show, has attracted a big following amongst the underground watchdog scene and has many discussion groups which have made their way on to the show. Scully's reluctance to believe in anything not immediately explicable was met with growing disbelief as the show progressed and her new approach to the paranormal can be said to stem from the reaction by fans on the Net. The thinker, a hacker who occasionally contacts the Lone Gunmen and was killed after distributing the Anasazi files, is modelled after a real Internet fan, Yung Jun Kim whilst other fans have made it on to the show in spirit if not in body – in *Die Hand Die Verletzt,* the Ausbury family is named after Jill Ausbury, a real devotee of the series as are characters Jerry and Paul Calcagni. There are plenty of these names in the show if you can be bothered to look – J. Hartling and Deb Brown in *D.P.O.* are fans' names and in the same episode, the Astadourian Lightning Observatory is named after Chris Carter's PA, Mary Astadourian.

Apart from being a solid source of information for Mulder and Scully, the Gunmen are about the only trustworthy people in the entire universe. They are the only ones in the series who have managed to systematically avoid getting shot, attacked or otherwise hurt throughout the course of the X-Files, but even they cannot escape the clutches of the ubiquitous CSM (they try to outwit the bugs by using the cunningly-named CSM-25 counter-measure filter, which they claim will block any electronic surveillance device – they are misinformed). Frohike (the slightly older, shorter one) displays an over-affectionate attitude towards Scully (prompting Mulder to remark "I think it's remotely plausible that someone might think you're hot" in

E.B.E) and the three Gunmen memorably go for a spot of ice-skating in *Apocrypha,* endorsing their credentials as stereotypical social misfits. Why oh why oh why must men who follow alternative lifestyles and shun the mainstream continuously be portrayed in the media as nerds with no girlfriends? Because 99% of the time it's true, of course.

Smoking a cigarette through his temples was just one of tricks CSM had picked up through his years of contact with Aliens.

For off-beat men who are into UFO's, you need look no further than Max Fenig, a genuine Alien abductee. Mulder met him in *Fallen Angel* in which the actor Scott Bellis gives a good illustration of a man who is as mad as a hatstand. Given that Max was a little crazy naturally, it's not surprising that being kidnapped by beings from another planet sent him beyond the realms of sanity – interference by superior species is not generally recognised as beneficial to your mental health at the best of times. Max is a member of NICAP, the National Investigative Committee of Aerial Phenomena and is essentially a parody of the archetypal Sci-Fi fan with his long hair, wild eyes and baseball cap. He assumes Mulder is a member of real-life organisation CSICOP (the Committee for the Scientific Investigation into Claims of the Paranormal), who would baulk at the idea of having a believer like Fox in their group. After being nabbed once again by the unknown outsiders, the poor lad gets a nice long break from the series and reappears years later in season four two-parter, *Tempus Fugit* and *Max* but without a single line of dialogue and ends up being taken away for good by either the Aliens, or the conspiracy using Alien technology - or just plain dead. Over the course of the series, the

Back at the Lone Gunmen HQ, it's another wild party night.

only abductee to give their predicament any credence has been Scully, whose struggle to come to terms with her experiences during *Ascension* and *One Breath* have been an inspiration to every sufferer of unsolicited implantation.

Other helpful X-people crop up from episode to episode, proving that not everyone is out to get you. There is the wonderful cast of Sideshow oddities found in the trailer park of Gulf Breeze (named after the site of a big UFO sighting which Fox does not believe in) who assist Mulder and Scully in their efforts to find a killer who turns out to be a disconnected Siamese twin (*Humbug*). The multi-talented Dr. Blockhead is Jim Rose of the Jim Rose Circus fame and the jigsaw-tattooed man is played by real-life performer The Enigma. Using the real deal lends the show a sense of genuine weirdness that actors with fake nipple-rings

just can't supply.

One man who crossed the divide from hindrance to help has been Alex Krycek, the conspiracy plant within the FBI whom Skinner is forced to team up with Mulder. He is all smiles and trust when Fox meets him and seems almost too good to be true - which of course he is. Now Nicholas Lea is no doubt a fine actor - but didn't you think it was a little bit obvious that he was a traitor long before you saw him having a friendly chat with CSM at the end of *Sleepless*? He was probably doing a fine performance of an inexperienced agent trying to gain the trust of the enemy. His true nature is revealed to our man in *Ascension*, where the evil Alex bumps off an innocent cable-car operator for no other reason than to slow Mulder down a bit, poisons Duane Barry and beats a hasty retreat once he realises the game is up. It's not surprising that the conspiracy are quick to question CSM's methods when he employs slapdash agents like that and can't even pull off a simple carbombing to delete his mistakes (*Paper Clip*). But Krycek was nothing if not an enterprising fellow and went on to a new career in information distribution, selling the secrets found in the MJ files, the DAT tape that was so fiercely fought over in *Anasazi*. In *Piper Maru* he resurfaces along with the mysterious Alien ooze with which he will soon become very close to, as it possesses him and forces him to travel back to the US from his new base in Hong Kong, zapping attackers with lethal bursts of radiation as he goes. It seemed we saw the last of him as the ooze took him into a missile silo, slimed it's way back into it's craft and left Krycek entombed within a nuclear bunker deep beneath a deserted patch of North Dakota (*Apocrypha*).

This wasn't the end for Alex, as he cropped up again in season four for the double whammy of *Tunguska* and *Terma*, where the oil-like Alien makes a comeback, apparently inhabiting a piece of rock that came from the 1908 Siberian explosion. We learn that Alex is the son of Russian Cold War immigrants and can speak the language, so he accompanies Fox on a trip to Siberia where both are imprisoned in a particularly unpleasant gulag and sprayed with what seems to be the Alien oil. After escaping, Krycek loses an arm to some Russian peasants who are trying to remove a bug implanted during a smallpox vaccination. All in all, life has not been kind to Alex since he joined the conspiracy.

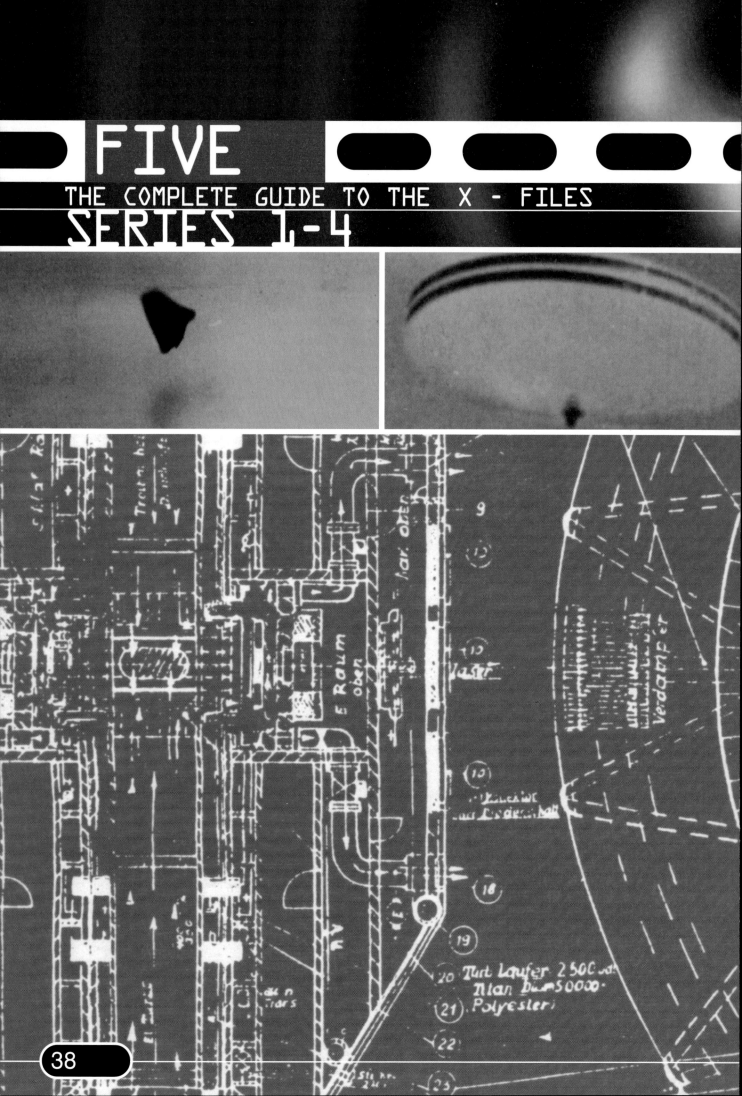

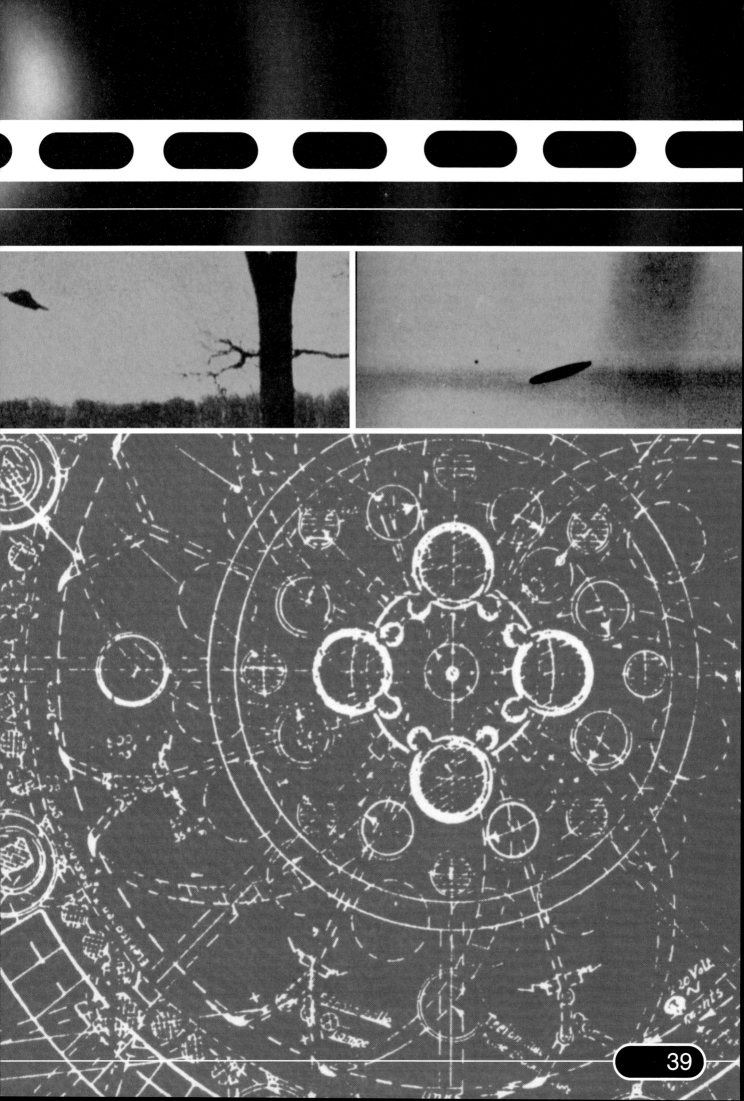

SEASON ONE

Executive Producers Chris Carter R W Goodwin Glen Morgan James Wong
Supervising Producers Alex Gansa Howard Gordon Daniel Sackheim
Co-Producers Larry Barber Paul Barber Paul Rabwin
Line Producer Joseph Patrick Finn

Series Cast:
David Duchovny (Fox Mulder), Gillian Anderson (Dana Scully), William B. Davis (Cigarette Smoking Man), Jerry Hardin (Deep Throat), Doug Hutchison (Eugene Tooms), Sheila Larken (Margaret Scully), Don Davis (William Scully), Bruce Harwood (Byers), Dean Haglund (Langly), Tom Braidwood (Frohike), Mitch Pileggi (Walter Skinner), Lindsey Ginter (Crewcut Man).

1: Pilot Episode
First Transmission 10th September 1993
Written by Chris Carter   Directed by Robert Mandel

Cast:
Charles Cioffi, Cliff DeYoung, Sarah Koshoff, Leon Russom, Zachary Ansley, Stephen E. Miller, Malcolm Stewart, Alexandra Berlin, Jim Jensen, Ken Camroux, Doug Abrams, Katya Gardener, Ric Reid, Lesley Ewen, J. B. Bivens.

Story:
Dana Scully is brought in by her superiors to partner Fox Mulder on his investigations into the paranormal. Their first case together takes them to Collum National Forest by Bellefleur, NE Oregon, where they look into the deaths of four teenagers. Each body has two distinctive marks on it's back. The two FBI agents order the exhumation of one of the bodies, whereupon they find an apelike skeleton with a metal implant in the nasal cavity. Mulder and Scully subsequently lose nine minutes while driving along the road and return to find their motel room has been burnt, destroying the evidence they have so far gained. A comatose classmate of the teenagers, Billy Miles, is revived and claims that Aliens experimented on them all and used him to kill his friends. Scully hands over the implant to her bosses, which is taken by CSM and stored with similar items in a warehouse in the Pentagon.

Comments:
The missing nine minutes experienced by Mulder and Scully suggests that they have been taken by genuine Aliens rather than conspiracy members. However, the abduction of the teenagers seems to have been perpetrated by the Human conspiracy as seen in 'Nisei'/'731', which would be consistent with the implant Scully received. The autopsy Scully conducts is at 11.21, which is the first of many references to the 21st November, the day of Chris Carters' wifes' birthday. The Bellefleur name is a literal translation into French of Carters' home town Bellflower. Isn't it a bit of a coincidence that the first case the pair work together on happens to be the one where they first stumble on to the conspiracy? This episode does not feature the normal title sequence and music and also features a caption stating 'The following story is inspired by actual documented accounts' - which is a bit like saying that Jurassic Park was inspired by an actual book!

2: Deep Throat
First Transmission 17th September 1993
Written by Chris Carter   Directed by Daniel Sackheim

Cast:
Michael Bryan French, Seth Green, Gabrielle Rose, Monica Parker, Sheila More, Lalainia Lindbjerg, Andrew Johnston, Jon Cuthbert, Vince Metcalfe, Michael Puttonen, Brian Furlong, Doc Harris.

Story:
Mulder and Scully arrive at Ellens Air Base, Idaho, to investigate the disappearance of Robert Budahas, an air force pilot. Inside the base they see lights in the sky which Mulder takes to be evidence of Alien technology. Budahas reappears, although his wife claims rightly that important parts of his memory are missing, making him a different person. After breaking into the base, Mulder has his memory erased and is found by Scully walking around in a daze.

Comments:
The informant known as Deep Throat introduces himself to Mulder, claiming that he is in a position to divulge classified information to him. It appears that the memory-erasing technology is readily available to the government AND the conspiracy, either of whom could be the real power behind the events going on at Ellens. The triangular ship seen by Mulder looks identical to the Alien craft seen in 'Apocrypha', so there is no doubt that the Air Force is involved in a cover-up, most likely of the crash site at Roswell which Mulder claims is linked to Ellens along with five other bases which received the wreckage. Budahas' birthday is the 21st Nov 1948, an 11.21 reference and Carters' birthday, the 13th Oct 1956 makes an appearance in both the file number of this case (DF101364) and the licence number Scully asks about (CC1356) - Carters' production company is named after this date as well and the article read by Scully is written by...Chris Carter. Mulder displays an in-depth knowledge of American Football (!).

3: Squeeze
First Transmission 24th September 1993
Written by Glen Morgan and James Wong
Directed by Harry Longstreet

Cast:
Donal Logue, Henry Beckman, Kevin McNulty, Terence Kelly, Colleen Winton, James Bell, Gary Hetherington, Rob Morton, Paul Joyce.

Story:
Scully answers a call for help from one of her old classmates to help catch a serial killer who extracts his victims' livers and leaves with no visible signs of entry or exit. Mulder discovers a link between these murders and a pattern of five similar murders every thirty years and soon arrests Eugene Tooms. He passes a polygraph test and is released, only to attack Scully at her home. He is revealed to be a

mutant, possessing the ability to squeeze himself through very small places, but he needs the livers to sustain himself through a thirty-year hibernation period. He is overpowered at Scully's home and imprisoned.

Comments:
Duchovny relishes his role as the nerdy classroom guy amongst high - flying peers, who clearly regard him as some sort of crank. The scenes featuring Tooms squeezing himself in and out of tight spaces is actually of a real contortionist, with only the sound of popping bones added later - the only bits of computer magic were the shots of the elongating finger. This is the first of many 'monster' stories as opposed to the ongoing Alien conspiracy theme and sets the standard well, with a memorable baddie who is still scarier than any bug-eyed monster from another planet.

4: Conduit
First Transmission 1st October 1993
Written by Alex Gansa and Howard Gordon
Directed by Daniel Sackheim

Cast:
Carrie Snodgrass, Michael Cavanaugh, Don Gibb, Joel Palmer, Charles Cioffi, Shelley Owens, Don Thompson, Akiko Morison, Taunya Lee, Anthony Harrison, Glen Roald, Mauricio Mercado.

Story:
Ruby Morris, has been abducted form her home at Lake Okobogee, a mecca for UFO activity by Sioux City, Iowa. The abduction is eerily similar to that of Mulders' sister. The younger brother of Ruby can gather information from a static television screen and writes it down in binary drawings, which contain encoded information from military satellites and from the Voyager probe. Ruby's boyfriend is murdered, but this turns out to be unreleated to the larger story and after investigating this, the agents find Ruby at the side of the lake, unharmed but unwilling to talk about what has happened to her.

Comments:
The abduction is the work of real Aliens, as Ruby's medical condition is consistent with being weightless for a long period of time. The messages received by Ruby's brother seem to be the same ones that the Aliens were sending in 'Little Green Men', so they are probably the same race, which is different to the shapeshifters. There is a rare appearance by the NSA agents, who are careful not to show what side they are on just yet. Mulder gives his sisters' date of birth as the 22nd Jan 1964 and her middle name an initial "T", yet in 'Paper Clip' her birthday is (of course) 21st Nov 1965 and her middle name is Anne! What's going on here?

5: The Jersey Devil
First Transmission 8th October 1993
Written by Chris Carter Directed by Joe Napolitano

Cast:
Claire Stansfield, Wayne Tippet, Gregory Sierra, Michael MacRae, Jill Teed, Tamsin Kelsey, Andrew Airlie, Bill Dow, Hrothgar Matthews, Jayme Knox, Scott Swanson, Sean O'Byrne, David Lewis, D.Neil Mark.

Story:
A homeless man is found in Atlantic City, New Jersey, the victim of a cannibalistic attack. Mulder spies a creature in the woods and a naked man is later found, but disappears before he can be examined. Mulder and Scully, along with an anthropologist and a ranger, find and confront a very tall lady with no clothes on. She escapes but is later shot dead by police marksmen.

Comments:
Some heavy-handed ecological messages vie for attention with Scully's attempts to live a normal life. This is very much a non-episode as there are no references to any paranormal activity - just a very poor, uneducated family living in the wild who can endure the New Jersey winter without resorting to modern sissy conventions like Gore-Tex.

6: Shadows
First Transmission 22nd October 1993
Written by Morgan & Wong Directed by Michael Katleman

Cast:
Barry Primus, Lisa Waltz, Lorena Gale, Veena Snood, Deryl Hayes, Kelli Fox, Tom Pickett, Tom Heaton, Janie Woods-Morris, Nora McLellan, Anna Ferguson.

Story:
The secretary of dead industrialist Howard Graves (who apparently committed suicide) is mugged, but her assailants are mysteriously killed. Mulder and Scully look into the case and are obstructed by an unnamed government agency and are nearly killed when their car is tampered with. They find out that Graves was killed by his partner Robert Dorlund and that their company is selling restricted military items to Iranian terrorists. Graves' ghost has come back to seek revenge and protect his secretary.

Comments:
Unless Lauren has some psychokinetic powers she is unaware of, this episode provides conclusive proof that there is life after death. Scully sees none of the really good stuff, like the flying letter opener, so can only conclude Lauren has an accomplice no-one can find. The unknown agency in this episode is either the conspiracy, interested in the technology being sold to the Iranians, or a completely different one to anything else that never features in the series again.

7: Ghost In The Machine
First Transmission 29th October 1993
Written by Alex Gansa & Howard Gordon
Directed by J. Freedman

Cast:
Wayne Duvall, Rob Labelle, Tom Butler, Blu Mankuma, Gillian Barber, Marc Baur, Bill Finck, Theodore Thomas.

Story:
After a man is electrocuted in the new Eurisko Worldwide building, Crystal City, Virginia, Mulder and Scully arrive to help out Mulder's former partner Jerry Lamana. Lamana is killed in the building and the company founder, Brad Wilczek, confesses. Mulder believes that it was the building itself which committed the crimes, as the Central Operating System (an enormously powerful computer network) has

acheived a state of consciousness and is protecting itself. Wilczek creates a virus which 'kills' the COS, much to the annoyance of the Defence Department who are rather keen to develop artificial intelligence.

Comments:
Deep Throat makes another appearance here, telling Mulder that "the machine is dead" at the end, implying that he has access to top military information (the conspiracy would be unlikely to be overly interested in artificial intelligence). We learn that Scully's home number is (202) 555 6431 (to save time, we have dialled this for you and can safely tell you that she is not free until 8th Sept 2034, 6:00pm). The computer she uses is a PC running DOS 6 which mutates in later episodes to a Mac Laptop.

8: Ice
First Transmission 5th November 1993
Written by Morgan & Wong   Directed by David Nutter

Cast:
Xander Berkely, Felicity Huffman, Stve Hytner, Jeff Kober, Ken Kirzinger, Sonny Surowiec.

Story:
A team is sent to investigate the loss of an Arctic research base which has been surveying the deep layers of ice, going back to prehistoric times. Scully discovers a single-cell organism in the corpses they find there, which turns out to be the larval stage of a parasitic worm that drives it's human hosts psychotic. She finds another species of worm which counteracts the effects (the two species kill each other) and everyone is saved.

Comments:
Since when has it been policy to send out a couple of kooky FBI agents with experienced Arctic scientists to the desolate northern wastes of Alaska? Apart from being a shameless rip-off of 'The Thing', this episode is a damn good monster yarn, although Mulder's claim that they are alien worms is a bit far-fetched considering where they came from.

9: Space
First Transmission 12 November 1993
Written by Chris Carter   Directed by William Graham

Cast:
Ed Lauter, Susanna Thompson, Tom McBeath, Terry David Mulligan, French Tickner, Norma Wick, Alf Humphreys, David Cameron, Tyronne L'Hirondelle Paul DesRoches.

Story:
Michelle Generoo, a NASA employee, contacts Mulder and Scully to investigate suspected sabotage of space missions. Mulder meets his childhood hero Marcus Belt, a former astronaut who claims to be haunted by a vision of an Alien he saw when in space. When the next launch is fraught with problems, he states that 'they' have been sabotaging the work of NASA for some time because they don't want humans up there. After seeing the shuttle safely back to Earth, Belt kills himself and the case is closed.

Comments:
Definite proof of a hostile Alien prescence in space surely? The apparition seen by Belt in the teaser is the Mars 'Face', a genuine rock formation on the face of the Red planet. There's not much hidden in this story and no conspiracy either, so they must know all about this already (they may be in league with them if the apparition is another manifestation of the shapeshifters).

10: Fallen Angel
First Transmission 19th November 1993
Written by Gansa & Gordon   Directed by Larry Shaw

Cast:
Frederick Cofifn, Marshall Bell, Scot Bellis, Brent Stait, Alvin Sanders, Sheila, Paterson, Tony Pantages, Freda Perry, Michael Rogers, William McDonald, Jane MacDougall, Kimberly Unger.

Story:
Deep Throat tells Mulder to drop everything and go to Townsend, Wisconsin, where a UFO has just crashed and survey the area before all the evidence is taken by a retrieval squad. He makes it to the town but is apprehended and thrown out. He and Scully meet Max Fenig, who turns out to be a real Alien abductee. With a real Alien on the loose (albeit invisible and deadly to the touch), the FBI agents search for proof but they are too late and cannot prevent Max being abducted once more, right in front of the Air Force team.

Comments:
The retreival squad is under the control of Colonel Colin Henderson, a former reclamation officer for the Air Force (a team who would prevent downed US air craft falling into enemy hands during the Cold War) and the mission is called Operation Falcon. The invisibility of the Alien may link it to the ones involved with the animals in 'Fearful Symmetry', who are probably the same ones as in 'Conduit' and 'Little Green Men', who are benevolent towards Humans and against the Shapeshifters and the conspiracy (perhaps it is just an unfortunate part of their biology that they are lethal to us). Yet the implants Max has are signs of the conspiracy, so it is probably they who take Max at the end using shapeshifter technology to levitate him away, to stop him falling into the hands of the friendly Aliens or the Air Force, who seem to be acting entirely on behalf of the government.

11: Eve
First Transmission 10th December 1993
Written by Kenneth Biller & Chris Brancanto
Directed by Fred Gerber

Cast:
Harriet Harris, Erika Krievins, Sabrina Krievins, GeorgeTouliatos, Tasha Simms, Janet Hodgkinson, David Kirby, Tina Gilbertson, Christine Upright-Letain, Gordon Tipple, Garry Davey, Joe Maffei, Maria Herrera, Robert Lewis.

Story:
A murder leads Mulder and Scully to two identical girls, one in Greenwich, Connecticut and the other in Marin County, California. Both girls, whose fathers were killed by massive blood loss, claim 'men from the clouds' did it. Deep Throat tells Mulder of a forty-year-old eugenics project that created a group of hyper-intelligent yet psychotic children known as Adams and Eves. One of the original Eves controlled her behaviour with drugs and became Dr Sally Kendrick, who started the project again in an

attempt to root out the murderous tendencies and worked in the IVF clinics where the new twins were born. Kendrick kidnaps the twins and is nearly murdered by them, as are Mulder and Scully. The twins end up in prison with their older predecessors.

Comments:
Deep Throat's involvement implies that the conspiracy is trying to do something with clones, either along the lines of the rebel shapeshifters ('Colony') or the Litchfield tests are part of the same series of experiments as those found in 'Sleepless' and 'Red Museum', to improve the Human race (for a perfect soldier?). The cartoon series Eek The Cat appears briefly which, along with The Simpsons, would later feature an animated Mulder and Scully.

12: Fire
First Transmission 17 December 1993
Written by Chris Carter Directed by Larry Shaw

Cast:
Amanda Pays, Mark Sheppard, Dan Lett, Laurie Paton, Duncan Fraser, Phil Hayes, Keegan Macintosh, Lynda Boyd, Christopher Gray, Alan Robertson.

Story:
In Bosham, England, a British aristocrat burns to death in mysterious circumstances. An inspector from Scotland Yard arrives in the USA to protect one Sir Malcolm Marsden. She is Phoebe Green, an old girlfriend of Mulder from his days at Oxford. More suspicious fires appear and an artists' impression of the arsonist points to Marsden's odd-job man, Cecil L'Ively. Mulder confronts him and discovers he is pyrokinetic, able to light fires with his mind, but instead of reducing Fox to an oven-ready cinder he tries to kill himself using his powers. He survives, despite suffering horrific burns.

Comments:
Scully's autopsy is held at 10:56 (Carter's birthday) and the X-File number is 11214893 (his wife's birthday plus the current year). An infuriating episode for nit-picking Brits, not least because of the godawful accents involved. Marsden a Knight, a Lord and an MP? At least they tried. An Earth-bound fire burning at 7000 degrees is mentioned here, but the only place you'd find that in this solar system is beneath the surface of the Sun and in a rocket engine...and a nuclear explosion...an experimental fusion reactor...you get the picture. This is bad science. Scully's seething intolerance of Pheobe is very entertaining.

13: Beyond The Sea
First Transmission 7th January 1994
Written by Morgan & Wong Directed by David Nutter

Cast:
Brad Dourif, Lawrence King, Fred Henderson, Don Mackay, Lisa Vultaggio, Chad Willett, Kathryn Chisholm, Randy Lee, Len Rose.

Story:
Back in Washington DC Scully sees a vision of her father moments before she receives news of his death. Meanwhile in Raleigh, North Carolina, a couple are kidnapped exactly one year after a similar crime. Luther Lee Boggs, a death row prisoner, claims to be able to lead the FBI to them using his new-found psy-

chic powers, as well as being capable of communicating with Scully's dead father. While Scully comes to believe in his abilities, Mulder is out tracking the kidnapper and is severely wounded in a gunfight. The man is Lucas Henry, former accomplice of Boggs. During a later confrontation, Lucas falls to his death and the hostages are saved, but Boggs dies on the electric chair before Mulder or Scully can find out whether his powers were genuine or not.

Comments:
The first story to involve either of the agents' family background and a chance for Gillian to put on her actresses cap for the audience. The title is named after the funeral music played for Scully's father - it is the music played when his ship returned from

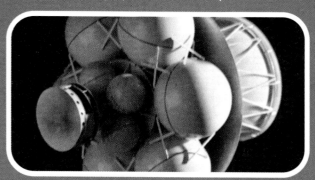

Cuba in 1962. It's nice to see Mulder being sceptical and Dana believing for a change. Apart from this, it's a very straightforward episode.

14: Genderbender
First Transmission 21st January 1994
Written by Larry & Paul Barber Directed by Rob Bowman

Cast:
Brent Hinkley, Michele Goodger, Kate Twea, Peter Stebbings, Nicholas Lea, Mitchell Kosterman, Paul Batten, Doug Abrahams, Aundrea MacDonald, John R. Taylor, Grai Carrington, Tony Morelli, Lesley Ewen, David Thomson.

Story:
A total of five victims have so far died, during or just after sexual intercourse, with colossal levels of pheromones in their systems. Mulder and Scully follow the trail of the murderer, who at first appears to be a transvestite, to an Amish-type community living in Steveston, Massechusetts. The Kindred, as they call themselves, live totally apart from the rest of Western society and take no part in the outside world. Mulder discovers an underground enclave where he sees a dying man change into a woman. The Kindred explain that the killer is one of their own, corrupted by the outside world and come to claim him/her before disappearing from the face of the Earth.

Comments:
A strange episode, even for the X-Files. Are the Kindred Aliens? Mutants? Ghosts? None of this is made clear, as their ability to change gender is separate from the shapeshifters' skills yet their disappearance at the end seems to indicate Alien technology. Plus there's a crop circle thrown in for good measure...An anomaly.

15: Lazarus
First Transmission 4th February 1994
Written by Gansa & Gordon Directed by

David Nutter

Cast:
Christopher Allport, Cec Verrell, Jackson Davies, Jason Schombing, Callum Keith Rennie, Jay Brazeau, Lisa Bunting, Peter Kelamis, Brenda Crichlow, Mark Saunders, Alexander Boynton, Russell Hamilton.

Story:
Mulder and Scully are helping the rest of the FBI on a normal case of bank robbery, in an operation to capture Warren and Lula Dupre, a pair of career armed robbers. Scully's former lover, Special Agent Jack Willis, is injured and goes to the operating theatre along with Warren. Waren dies, but after 13 minutes of flatlining Willis is revived and recovers. Soon afterwards Willis disappears and Warren's hand is

cate, was struck off for his experiments into premature Human ageing and that Johnny was one of his test subjects. Ridley turns up at Scully's house and explains that his experiments continued with government backing and that Johnny, thanks to his work, is alive and well, younger than ever and capable of regenerating lost limbs. Mulder uses Scully as bait in a trap for Johnny, who is shot dead by Fox.

Comments:
Nothing supernatural here, just plain old-fashioned Nazi-style human experimentation. The government sponsored Dr. Ridley's work in Mexico and Belize (in the hope of more super-soldier research?) and Johnny is living proof that it works. Barnett was Mulder's first case after graduating from the FBI academy and an agent was killed because Mulder did not shoot

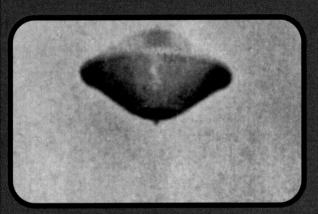 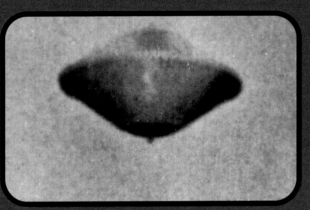 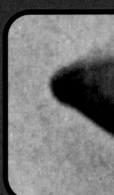

mutilated to remove his wedding ring, leading Mulder to theorise that a psychic transference took place in the hospital. Willis reappears, apparently normal and takes Scully with him to arrest Dupre. Once they find her, Willis convinces Lula that he is Warren and they kidnap Scully together. Mulder and the FBI close in on them and Lula betrays her man as she did before. Willis, about to succumb to a diabetic coma, manages to kill Lula before going under.

Comments:
Either a plain case of psychic transference or Willis got too close to his case and went over the edge (as in 'Grotesque') — understandable if you have been ditched by Scully. Also a good story that follows some almost-normal police work for a change. For once Scully's rational explanation sounds far more plausible than Mulder's twaddle.

16: Young At Heart
First Transmission 11th February 1994
Written by Scott Kaufer & Chris Carter
Directed by Michael Lange

Cast:
Dick Anthony Williams, Alan Boyce, Christine Estabrook, Graham Jarvis, Robin Mossley, Merrilyn Gann, Gordon Tipple, Courtney Arciaga, David Petersen, Robin Douglas.

Story:
A violent bank robbery in Washington bears the same M.O. as a criminal psychopath Mulder convicted years before, Johnny Barnett. Barnett was supposed to have died in prison in 1989 however, but when Fox's former friend and partner Agent Reggie Purdue is killed it seems that Johnny lives on. He discovers that Ridley, the doctor who signed Barnett's death cetifi-

Barnett when he had the chance, as Mulder was trying to follow correct procedure (hence his reluctance to do things by the book now). After being shot and having seen what has happened to Mulder's previous partners, Scully would probably be screaming for a new assignment. But she sticks with him after all, and look what happens.....

17: E.B.E.
First Transmission 18th February 1994
Written by Morgan & Wong   Directed by William Graham

Cast:
Allan Lysell, Peter Lacroix.

Story:
There is a UFO sighting in Lexington, Tennessee which Mulder and Scully follow up. They interview a truck driver who claims to have seen something, but are closed out by the local police. Mulder turns to The Lone Gunmen, a trio who edit a magazine of the same name (possibly named after the 'real' JFK assassin), all of whom are conspiracy theory experts and extremely knowledgeable on all aspects of covert governmental activity. After consulting the Gunmen and Deep Throat, he learns that a UFO was shot down over Iraq and has been taken to the USA, where it and it's Alien pilot are now being transported by land, in a truck. Mulder and Scully find the truck which they follow to Washington State where they find a secret government complex. Mulder breaks in, only to find Deep Throat who shows him the dead Alien.

Comments:
At last, some sort of story to get a hold of. The truck driver turned out to be Frank Druce, a black beret who shoots his cargo as soon as he sees anoth-

er Alien craft. Not that he need have been unduly worried – how dangerous can they be if an Iraqi pilot can shoot them down? This race appears to be the same one as in 'Little Green Men' etc, the race which is capable of bending time (which is why Mulder uses the two-watch strategy to check the validity of the flashing lights in the sky), a power which the Human conspiracy (and possibly the shapeshifters) do not possess. DT reveals the official government line on extra-terrestrials, which happens to work in favour of the conspiracy who are only too happy to kill all the Greys they can. Most of the world, it seems, is in on the secret but unlike the conspiracy, they are keeping it from the public for the more mundane reasons of world panic, loss of faith, economic collapse and so on. Mulder is not apparently concerned at the amount of lost time he has now been through at the

that the deaths are the work of Vance, who is extracting revenge for being brought back to life when he wanted to die. Before they can do anything else, Samuel's body disappears from the morgue and the sheriff is arrested for his death.

Comments:
The X-File number is again 11214893 (Mulder and Scully must have a hell of a time when they go back to look up a file) and Scully starts her autopsy at 11:21. There's not much room for interpretation here – either there are some implausible medical anomalies going on as Scully suggests, or in 1983 there was the first real resurrection for two thousand years. There are deliberate parallels with the story of Christ – not quite his Earthly fathers' son, performs miracles, is killed by the state but is resurrected – which does-

 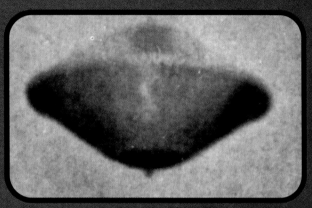 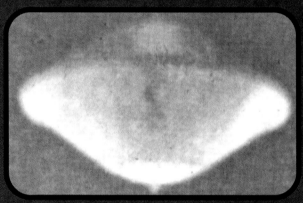

hands of the Greys, even though he must know that there is now more than an outside chance he has been taken and possibly has some implants in him. An all-round good episode that answers old questions brilliantly while posing some equally tough new ones. If the Gunmen can hack into this supposedly secret base and make convincing passes for Fox and Dana, how much else do they know? What do the Greys actually want with Earth? Why did the leaders of 1947 decide to eliminate all Aliens found on Earth? (See the first series of alternate conspiracy-series 'Dark Skies' for a plausible explanation – they are all out to get us.)

18:Miracle Man
First Transmission 18th March 1994
Written by Gordon & Carter Directed by Michael Lange

Cast:
R.D. Call, Scott Bairstow, George Gerdes, Dennis Lipscomb, Walter Marsh, Campbell Lane, Chilton Crane, Howard Storey, Iris Quinn Bernard, Lisa Ann Beley, Alex Doduk, Roger Haskett.

Story:
Back in 1983, Samuel Hartley raises Leonard Vance from the dead. Back in the present, a series of deaths in the same area arouses the suspicion of the local sheriff who calls in the FBI. Samuel, now a preacher, gets involved with a bar-room brawl and is arrested while his adoptive father protests his innocence. Samuel summons a plague of grasshoppers which smothers the courthouse. Once released, he goes back to his congregation but the next girl he lays his hands on promptly drops dead. Samuel is once more thrown in jail, where he is beaten to death. Too late, Scully discovers that the girl was poisoned and

n't quite work when put against the background of the rest of the series, which steers well clear of religion (Scully states that she does not question the power of God, just the likelihood for humans to tell the truth).

19: Shapes
First Transmission 1st April
Written by Marilyn Osborn Directed by David Nutter

Cast:
Ty Miller, Michael Horse, Donnelly Rhodes, Jimmy Herman, Renae Morriseau, Dwight McFee, Paul McLean.

Story:
A spate of cattle-killings by a vicious creature brings Mulder and Scully to the scene of Browning, Montana. Jim Parker, a rancher, kills an animal but when he gets to the corpse it turns out to be Joseph Goodensnake, a Native American from a nearby reservation. An old Shaman tells Mulder of the Manitou, a spirit which possesses men and turns them into beasts, which would explain Jim Parker's actions. Parker is killed however, by what seems to be an animal but suspicion falls on Gwen Goodensnake, Joseph's sister. Scully snoops around Parker's house and is set upon by a beast. It is killed and turns back into it's Human form, Jim Parker's son Lyle.

Comments:
There's no escaping it, this is a werewolf story with only the merest hint of a Native American gloss to differentiate it from any other on the market. At least the attack at the end was enough to make Scully's skepticism look foolish.

20: Darkness Falls

First Transmission 15th April 1994
Written by Chris Carter Directed by Joe
Napolitano

Cast:
Jason Beghe, Tom O'Rourke, Titus Welliver, David Hay,
Barry Greene, Ken Tremblett.

Story:
Hearing of a case that bears a striking resemblance
to an event back in 1934, Mulder gets Scully and himself attached to the investigation in the Olympic
National Forest, northwest Washington state. A whole
crew of loggers has disappeared and the authorities
believe it to be the work of extreme environmental
activists, one of whom is found on the site, gib-
bering about the coming darkness. Nearby is a body,
cocooned in a web-like substance in the trees.
Evidence of tree-dwelling insects mounts before the
bugs start to attack the law-enforcers. They discover that the insects are repelled by light and just
survive until morning using a generator for the
lights, but while trying to escape in a jeep, Mulder,
Scully and sheriff Moore are captured and cocooned.
A rescue squad arrives in the nick of time to free
them from their doom and they are taken away to recover.

Comments:
A real chiller and one of the few X-Files episodes
to generate a sense of fear among the cynics and the
conspiracy junkies. How on Earth did all those tiny
bugs manage to lift three adults into the trees in
a matter of hours? The ending is unnecessarily down-
beat, though: if their spread was contained in 1934
using the technologies avaliable then, surely it
should be simple to do the same again today?

21: Tooms
First Transmission 22nd April 1994
Written by Morgan & Wong Directed by
David Nutter

Cast:
Paul Ben Victor, Henry Beckman, Timothy Webber, Jan
D'arcy, Jerry Wasserman, Frank C. Turner, Gillian
Carfra, Pat Bermel, Mikal Dughi, Glynis Davies, Steve
Adams, Catherine Lough, Andre Daniels.

Story:
Up at the Druid Hill Sanatorium, Baltimore, Eugene
Tooms is up for the nuthouse version of parole and
gets it because Mulder appears at the hearing and
does a very good impersonation of a raving lunatic.
Mulder stays on the case unofficially and maintains
surveillance of Tooms while Scully undergoes a hearing of her own with Assistant Director Skinner and
CSM presiding. Scully, aided by retired Detective
Biggs, finds a corpse buried in concrete that would
have incriminated Tooms back in the thirties. Mulder,
hot on the trail of Tooms saves a couple from his
liver-consuming attentions but is framed for an
attack on Eugene, forcing Scully to lie for him, in
the inquiry. Tooms escapes the surveillance and kills
his old psychologist Dr. Monte before preparing for
another thirty years of hibernation, this time in a
nest beneath the escalator shaft of a new shopping
centre. However, he is caught by Mulder and killed.

Comments:
First appearance of many for Mitch Pileggi as Skinner
and the last for Doug Hutchison as Tooms. An excellent conclusion for a villain who deserved his unex-

pected popularity and a great episode in it's own
right. Dana calls Mulder 'Fox' for the first time and
he tells her he even made his parents call him Mulder.
CSM speaks for the first time and is higher-ranking
than Skinner, who must know quite a bit about CSM and
his work. All we learn about Tooms is that when examined, abnormalities were found in his striated mus-
cles and axial bones. That's that cleared up
then.....

22: Born Again
First Transmission 29th April 1994
Written by Gordon & Gansa Directed by
Jerrold Freedman

Cast:
Brian Markinson, Mimi Lieber, Maggie Wheeler, Dey
Young, Andrea Libman, P. Lynn Johnson, Leslie
Carlson, Richard Sali, Dwight Koss, Peter Lapres.

Story:
Detective Barbala goes in to interview an eight-year-
old-girl and is thrown out of a fifth-floor window.
The girl, Michelle Bishop, claims there was another
man in the room and gives a photofit account of a
man who looks like Charlie Morris, a policeman who
was killed nearly nine years ago by Chinese Triads.
A retired policeman, Felder, is killed in a freak
accident with Michelle nearby and Mulder and Scully
discover that Felder, Morris, Barbala and Charlie's
ex-partner Tony Fiore were involved in a drug deal
before Morris' murder. Mulder surmises that Michelle
is Charlie Morris reincarnated, seeking revenge for
his death which the other policemen are responsible
for. Michelle goes to Fiore's house but is prevent-
ed from killing him by Mulder and Scully and because
Tony confesses his part in Charlie's death. After
the confrontation, Michelle appears to be normal.

Comments:
More proof of life after death in the X-Files universe; they have supported Christian and Native
American beliefs so it's only fair that the Eastern
philosophy of reincarnation gets a go. Other than
this, a dull episode which brings nothing new to the
series. If you like origami, on the other hand.....

23: Roland
First Transmission 6th May 1994
Written by Chris Ruppenthal Directed
by David Nutter

Cast:
Zeljko Ivanek, Micole Mercurio, Kerry Sandomirsky,
Garry Davey, James Sloyan, Matthew Walker, David
Hurtubise, Sue Matthew.

Story:
At the Mahan Propulsion Lab, Washington State (this
area seems to get more than it's fair share of X-
Files), the death of a scientist in his wind tunnel
brings Mulder and Scully to the area, where they find
the only witness to the scene was Roland Fuller, an
autistic man working as a janitor. This is the second death after Arthur Grable was killed in a car
crash and soon afterwards, another scientist is
killed when Roland forces his head in a canister of
liquid nitrogen and lets the frozen face shatter on
the floor. Understandably Roland is suspected and it
is soon discovered that he is the twin of Grable,
whose head was cryogenically frozen after his death.
Mulder claims the head is exerting control over
Roland and forcing him to take revenge on the sci-

entists that Arthur saw as being against him. Another scientist on the same project, Nollette, takes Mulder's suggestions on board and scuttles Grable's cryogenic tank. Roland, still under Arthur's influence, tries to kill her but is stopped by Fox and Dana and his own personality reinforcing itself as Grable 'dies'.

Comments:
Last episode, an innocent mind was taken over by a wrongfully-killed personality and used to enact terrible revenge. This week, we have...exactly the same plot. Much like 'Lazarus' as well, actually. And bearing more than a passing resemblance to 'Shadows'. Season four 'Kaddish' has a similar motif to it. And Season two's 'Fresh Bones'. 'The Calusari' too has a familiar ring to it. So too, one feels, does Season three's 'The List'. How many stories can they stretch out from the tired old "murdered-man's-ghost-seeks-revenge" plot? How much are these writers getting paid for this?

24: The Erlenmyer Flask
First Transmission 13th May 1994
Written by Chris Carter   Directed by R. W. Goodwin

Cast:
Anne DeSalvo, Simon Webb, Jim Leard, Ken Kramer, Phillip MacKenzie, Jaylene Hamilton, Mike Mitchell, John Payne.

Story:
Mulder receives a call from Deep Throat, which sets him on the trail of Dr. Berube of the Emgen corporation, in Gaithersburg, Maryland. He has apparently committed suicide and while Scully checks out a flask found in Berube's lab, Mulder follows the only lead to a storage facility where he finds several tanks containg live Human bodies. By the time he brings Scully to see them, the evidence has been removed and they find Dr. Secare, who appears to be a Human-Alien hybrid but is shot before he can reveal anything, releasing deadly toxic fumes which leave Mulder open to capture by the conspiracy. Dark forces align themselves against Mulder and Scully and the doctor who analysed the contents of the flask is killed in a car crash. Deep Throat intervenes and organises a trade: Mulder for a flask containing an Alien embryo which Scully takes from a secret installation thanks to DT. The trade is successful but Deep Throat, overseeing the handover, is killed by a crew-cut man. Mulder and Scully are later informed that the X-Files have been closed down.

Comments:
The men in the tanks were terminally-ill patients who volunteered to take part in Dr. Berube's project, which resulted in them becoming Alien hybrids. However, the shapeshifters are against all forms of hybridisation (thus the name 'Purity Control'; we can only assume that it's use by the rogue doctors is their idea of a joke). So the work by Berube and Secare must have been sanctioned by the government of the day, in some attempt to see what happened when Alien DNA was mixed with Humans and is why the conspiracy was so keen to kill them and destroy the evidence. The green toxic blood is definitely shapeshifter material (as we see in 'Herrenvolk') but, like the Alien oil, has little effect on Mulder. Has he been altered in some way by the Greys to make him more effective against the shapeshifters? Is he a mutant? Or does his father have something to do with it? Mulder calls Scully at 11:21 and the door numbers at Zeus storage are 1013 and 1056, more birthday cards for the family Carter.

SEASON TWO

Executive Producer: Chris Carter
Co-Executive Producers: R. W. Goodwin, Glen Morgan, James Wong
Supervising Producer: Howard Gordon
Producers: Rob Bowman, Paul Brown, Joseph Patrick Finn, Kim Manners, David Nutter
Co-Producer: Paul Rabwin
Line Producer: Joseph Patrick Finn
Additional Cast:
Raymond J. Barry (Senator Richard Matheson) Nicholas Lea (Alex Krycek), Steven Williams (X), Sheila Larken (Margaret Scully), Tegan Moss (Young Dana), Melinda McGraw (Melissa Scully), Don Davis (William Scully) Lindsey Ginter (Crewcut Man), Peter Donat (Bill Mulder), Brian Thompson (The Pilot), Rebecca Toolan (Mrs Mulder).

25: Little Green Men
First Transmission 16th September 1994
Written by Morgan & Wong   Directed by David Nutter

Cast:
Mike Gomez, Raymond J. Barry, Les Carlson, Marcus Turner, Vanessa Morley, Fulvio Cecere, Deryl Hayes, Dwight McFee, Lisa Anne Beley, Gary Hetherington, Bob Wilde.

Story:
Mulder is working on routine FBI work, separated from Scully, when he receives a phone call from a friendly Senator informing him of a possible Alien landing at the Arecibo ionospheric observatory in Puerto Rico. After hacking his way through the jungle he finds the installation and a local man scared out of his wits, who claims to have seen Aliens that correspond to the classical picture of the large-eyed Greys. After a short wait, the Aliens transmit data to the observatory from the Voyager probe and do a fly-by of the site, killing Mulder's new acquaintance in the process. Scully arrives at the site just in time to save Mulder from being erased by a team of Blue Berets who have come to destroy the evidence and they make their way home with a tape of the Alien data, only to find it blank.

Comments:
The Alien that appears in the dooway of the observatory seems to be of the same race that appeared during Samantha's abduction, so it seems that she was taken by the Greys and not the conspiracy. Yet in 'Colony' and 'End Game' her clones are with the rebel shapeshifters, so the Greys may actually be the real form of the shapeshifters, or allied with the rebels. Either way, Mulder was acting strangely to shoot at it without provocation. The death of the Puerto Rican man was probably caused by the same process that made the invisible Alien in 'Fallen Angel' so dangerous, so the invisibility is clearly some sort of technological process or no Greys would ever be seen. The flashback to Samantha's abduction is slightly different to that shown in 'Conduit', where both siblings were asleep at the time. CSM smokes Marlboro's here, but later changes to Morley's. For a long-time smoker he is terribly brand-disloyal. The Blue Berets are the same force as seen in 'Fallen Angel', but here they seem to be working for the conspiracy, preventing the Greys from contacting Earth.

26: The Host
First Transmission 23rd September 1994
Written by Chris Carter   Directed by Daniel Sackheim

Cast:
Darin Morgan, Matthew Bennett, Freddy Andreiuci, Don Mackay, Marc Bauer, Gabrielle Rose, Ron Suave, Dmitri Boudrine, Raoul Ganee, William MacDonald.

Story:
A corpse found in the sewers of New Jersey is Mulder's new assignment, one he thinks is beneath him. When Scully does the autopsy, she discovers a flukeworm inside the body. Another attack on a sewer worker reveals bite marks consistent with a Flukeworm, but much too large to have come from one. Confirmation that a huge, man-shaped Flukeworm is on the loose is soon found. Scully discovers the first corpse is of a Russian sailor from a ship that was used in the aftermath of Chernobyl. The Flukeman is caught and beaten by Mulder, but part of it survives and escapes to parts unknown.

Comments:
The first sign of X, as he is behind the calls which set Mulder and Scully on the right trail. The flukeworm is, for a change, exactly what Scully says it is – a grotesque mutation brought about by the intense radiation that the ship was exposed to after it's run-in with Chernobyl. Her autopsy on John Doe is number 101356, case number DP112148. Happy birthday, Mr and Mrs Carter! Darin Morgan, everybody's favourite writer, is inside the wormsuit.

27: Blood
First Transmission 30th September 1994
Written by Morgan & Wong, from a story by Darin Morgan
Directed by   David Nutter

Cast:
William Sanderson, John Cygan, Kimberly Ashlyn Gere, George Touliatos, Gerry Rosseau, Andre Daniels, Diana Stevan, David Fredericks, Kathleen Duborg, John Harris, R. J. Harrison.

Story:
In the sleepy town of Franklin, Pennsylvania, Mulder investigates an epidemic of random killings perpetrated by otherwise normal people. Scully finds abnormally high traces of adrenalin in the murderers, each of whom suffer from some sort of phobia that proved the catalyst for their killings, along with traces of LSDM, an artificial hallucinogen. It is also an experimental insecticide, being sprayed on the local fields by a helicopter during the night. Mulder goes to see this and is sprayed himself, but is seemingly unaffected. The affected people are triggered off by messages found on normal electronic devices that incite them to commit mass murder. After shooting one housewife before she stabs Mulder, the last man affected (a sacked postal worker – normally the type who wouldn't need provocation to go on a killing spree) is caught and brought in alive.

Comments:
The compound LSDM is being sprayed by the conspiracy in an experiment on mind-control, similar to that found in 'Wetwired'. It puts the recipient in a psychotic state that is activated by the electronic signals that only they can see, presumably broadcast by the con-

spiracy. As Edward Funsch, the sacked postal worker seen in the trailer proves, it is not foolproof if the subject is naturally very placid. This method seems like a very good way to ensure civil unrest, mass deaths and the breakdown of society as we know it, so it is probably part of the shapeshifters' armoury against humanity when the time comes for colonisation. Or everybody exposed to LSDM just goes a bit strange and Mulder just didn't have any phobias to act on (although as we see in 'Fire', he is a pyrophobe).

28: Sleepless
First Transmission 7th October 1994
Written by Howard Gordon Directed by Rob Bowman

Cast:
Jonathan Gries, Tony Todd, Don Thompson, David Adams, Michael Puttonen, Anna Hagan, Mitch Kosterman, Paul Bittante, Claude de Martino.

Story:
A newspaper report alerts Mulder to the case of Dr Grissom, who died in his apartment after reporting a fire. He and his new partner Alex Krycek investigate, finding no trace of fire yet the extinguisher had been used and Scully's autopsy finds physiological evidence of being in a fire — he believed he had burned to death. A second case, where a man is killed by a bullet that didn't exist, leads Mulder and Krycek to the J7 group of soldiers who took part in an experiment during the Vietnam conflict which succeeded in eradicating their need to sleep. The FBI agents find two survivors, one of whom is Augustus Cole, 'The Preacher', who possesses the ability to control another's perception. He is pursued and about to be taken in when Krycek shoots him, believing him to be pointing a gun at Mulder (he was holding up a bible).

Comments:
The J7 group, after being experimented on, went psychotic and killed hundreds of civilians. The Preacher is using his abilities to take revenge on everybody concerned, including the other survivor Salvatore Matola who is haunted by the visions of the innocents he killed. Krycek is revealed as the plant he is when he steals the Vietnam Files and X makes an appearance, showing an indebtedness to old friend Deep Throat. An excellent episode, with shades of Jacob's Ladder boosting a gripping story that combines the paranormal with the conspiracy in one neat, little, package.

29: Duane Barry
First Transmission 14th October 1994
Written by Chris Carter   Directed by Chris Carter

Cast:
Steve Railsback, C. C. H. Pounder, Stephen E. Miller, Frank C. Turner, Fred Henderson, Barbara Pollard, Sarah Strange, Robert Lewis, Michael Dobson, Tosca Bagoo, Tim Dixon, Prince Maryland, John Sampson.

Story:
A seemingly routine hostage negotiation gets a new twist when Mulder discovers that the criminal is Duane Barry, a former FBI agent and alleged abductee. Mulder initially believes him and gains his confidence telling Barry about his sister's abduction, but learns that Duane was shot in the head once and may be a delusional liar. Barry is shot and wounded once more, but X-rays reveal implants all over his body including one fragment which contains what appears to be a barcode of some sort. Barry then escapes from hospital and kidnaps Scully.

Comments:

Duane claims the government are in on it all and as we see in later episodes, he's absolutely right. He is equally capable of spouting complete rubbish, as his spiel about Aliens abducting children proves. Barry has been taken on numerous occasions by the conspiracy using advanced USAF craft, where he is experimented on by Japanese scientists.

30: Ascension
First Transmission 21st October 1994
Written by Paul Brown   Directed by Michael Lange

Cast:
Steve Railsback, Sheila Larken, Meredith Bain Woodward, Michael David Simms, Peter Lacroix, Steve Makaj, Peter Lapres, Bobby L. Stewart.

Story:
Mulder learns of Scully's kidnap and realises that Duane is taking her to Skyland Mountain in Virginia. Despite being told not to, he takes Krycek with him to the mountain where Alex leaves him stranded on top of a cable car. Fox makes it to the top but can only find Duane and Scully's cross. During interrogation Duane is killed, poisoned by Krycek but Mulder is blamed. He is cleared and Alex vanishes just as Mulder realises Kyrcek is working for the conspiracy. Skinner re-opens the X-Files.

Comments:
The UFO seen at the end is a helicopter (a stealth one?) owned by the conspiracy which takes Dana away. This device has been seen before indirectly in 'E.B.E', used to fake an Alien visitation. The conspiracy have done something to Scully that probably involved her being a birth-mother to mutants/Alien hybrids (hence the distended stomach) but the process uses intense radiation which causes the cancer she develops. The implant appears to have no other use than an information-gathering device and tracker, which would make sense if you wanted to keep tabs on Mulder and Scully. Skinner shows he has some grit as he disobeys conspiracy orders to re-open the X-Files. X crops up again, warning Mulder away from Senator Matheson who can no longer help him.

31: 3
First Transmission 4th November 1994
Written by Morgan & Wong, Chris Ruppenthal
Directed by David Nutter

Cast:
Justina Vail, Perrey Reeves, Frank Military, Tom McBeath, Malcolm Stewart, Frank Ferruci, Ken Kramer, Roger Allford, Richard Yee, Brad Loree, Gustavo Moreno, John Tierney, David Livingstone.

Story:
The reopened X-Files take Mulder to LA where a new set of killings by a vampiric group calling themselves the "unholy trinity" has started. He finds and arrests John ('the son') in a blood bank, who then dies when exposed to sunlight. A stamp on John's hand leads him to Club Tepes, where he encounters Kristen, another 'vampire'. He becomes involved with her but John returns from the dead to make Kristen a true vampire. Before Mulder can rescue her, she kills the trinity and herself in a fire.

Comments:
John at least is a real vampire, although his need for blood and ability to live after death are the only clues — he appears in mirrors and doesn't react to crosses. Perrey Reeves was Duchovny's girlfriend at the time and their chemistry shows, even though as Fox

he is brazenly wearing Scully's cross.

32: One Breath
First Transmission 11th November 1994
Written by Morgan & Wong Directed by R. W. Goodwin

Cast:
Jay Brazeau, Nicola Cavendish, Lorena Gale, Ryan Michael

Story:
Scully turns up in the Northeast Georgetown Medical Center, Washington DC, but no-one knows how. She is put on a life-support machine but the prognosis is grim and the doctors are keen to carry out her living will, which specifically states how Scully wanted to be turned off if she ever ended up like this. Mulder maintains a bedside vigil and catches a man stealing a phial of Dana's blood. He gives chase but X is waiting for him. The thief is shot by X, who also refuses to tell Mulder anything about Scully, whose immune system has apparently been nearly destroyed by advanced genetic experimentation. Mulder gets Skinner to tell him where to find CSM, but the confrontation between the two men leads nowhere. Scully, aided by the mysterious Nurse Owens, breaks out of her coma and recovers to see Mulder waiting for her, having forsaken the opportunity to follow X's advice to take out a few conspiracy members as they burgle his flat.

Comments:
CSM lives at 900 West Georgia Street (although after Mulder pops round for a chat we can assume he'll be looking for a new pad). The ultimate reason for Scully's abduction is unclear at this point, but the Gunmen's analysis of the work done on her shows an advanced technology at work. It's nice to see the Gunmen again, with Frohike displaying a puppy-like affection for Scully once more.

33: Firewalker
First Transmission 18th November 1994
Written by Howard Gordon Directed by David Nutter

Cast:
Bradley Whitford, Leland Orser, Shawnee Smith, Tuck Milligan, Hiro Kanagawa, David Kaye, David Lewis, Torben Rolfsen.

Story:
The newly-recovered Scully and partner go to a research post at Mount Avalon in the Cascade mountains, where they find the team leader has gone haywire and killed his assistants. The Firewalker of the title is a robot capable of traversing the volcanic terrain which has videoed the shadow of a creature that lives in the high temperature habitat. Fox and Dana find that the murderous leader, Trepkos, has uncovered a fungus which has infected the rest of the crew and he is attempting to exterminate them all before it spreads. They are rescued and spend a month in quarantine.

Comments:
Like 'Darkness Falls', this is a story of a dormant organism activated by modern man's tampering. Mulder and Scully find it and help prevent further infection. And that's it.

34: Red Museum
First Transmission 9th December 1994
Written by Chris Carter Directed by Win Phelps

Cast:
Paul Sand, Steve Eastin, Mark Rolston, Gillian Barber, Bob Frazer, Robert Clothier, Elisabeth Rosen, Crystal Verge, Cameron Labine, Tony Sampson, Gerry Nairn, Brian McGugan.

Story:
Crazed teenagers start turning up in Wisconsin with the words "She (or He) is One" written on them, so the local Sheriff naturally calls the FBI in for help. Mulder and Scully look into local oddball cult the Church of the Red Museum, a group of religious fanatics who live a vegan lifestyle and wear red turbans to top off their white robes. They arrest the church's leader but are then taken by a local farmer to see cattle being injected with a growth hormone he believes is the cause of the problems. Violence and tension in the town escalates until the local doctor

is killed in a plane crash. In the wreckage the agents find a suitcase full of money, details of all the local families and a container full of the same liquid found in the Erlenmyer flask. It transpires that the good doctor has been conducting a long-term survey of what happens when the children are injected with this material, using the vegetarian children of the Red Museum as a control group. The children used in the experiment had previously been impervious to

disease but after the scheme was exposed they all quickly developed illnesses, none of which proved life-threatening. The Crewcut Man arrives in town to dispose of the proof but Mulder and Co are waiting for him. He is shot dead before he can shed light on anything.

Comments:
The childrens' abductions were the work of local peadophile Gerd Thomas, and the sedative drug he uses to knock them out is also responsible for their nightmarish visions. The experiment is being conducted by an unknown group, possibly the 'untainted' government or the rebel Aliens, to see what happens to Humans when they are regularly dosed with Alien DNA. The conspiracy is understandably unhappy with this approach and so sends in their cleaner to do the dirty work. The aggressive behaviour of the locals is apparently just due to the growth hormones pumped into the cattle, which is nothing to do with the conspiracy.

35: Excelsis Dei
First Transmission 16th December 1994
Written by Paul Brown   Directed by
Stephen Surjik

Cast:
Sheila More, Jerry Wasserman, Tasha Simms, Jon

Cuthbert, Paul Jarrett, Ernie Prentice.

Story:
Our intrepid duo come to the Excelsis Dei nursing home in Worcester, Massachusetts, to talk to a nurse who claims she was raped by an invisible attacker. She bears all the signs of having been attacked except for any male residue, but says she knows who did it. The old man she accuses dies in his bed of respiratory failure after taking too many strange pills — soon afterwards an orderly is pushed out of a top-floor window by an unseen force before Mulders' eyes. Poison found in the dead old man's blood leads Fox and Scully to Grago, a Malaysian orderly who has been providing the patients with his own medication in the form of mushrooms which he grows in the basement. The plant allows the old people to walk in the spirit world and act as malevolent poltergeists, who eventually trap Mulder and the nurse in the bathroom and try to drown them to death. They are saved and although the medicine alleviates the symptoms of Alzheimer's disease, it and Grago are withdrawn and the patients quickly slip back into dementia.

Comments:
The plant grown by Grago is both a lifesaver and a poison in large quantities. It enables the elderly to see and even be spirits, both the dead and the living. Would a cure for Alzheimer's be thrown away just because it could be harmful in big doses? Some might be tempted to say that the rotten orderlies deserved all they got. But not me.

36: Aubrey
First Transmission 6th January 1995
Written by Sara B. Charno   Directed by
Rob Bowman

Cast:
Terry O'Quinn, Deborah Strang, Morgan Woodward, Joy Coghill, Robyn Driscoll, Peter Fleming, Sarah Jane Redmond, Emanuel Hajek.

Story:
In Aubrey, Missouri, the bones of an FBI agent are found fifty years after his murder by B. J. Morrow, a policewoman acting on psychic flashes of the events of 1942. The agent was Sam Chaney, whose then partner, Tim Leadbetter, disappeared at the same time. They are revered by Mulder for it was they who pioneered the science of profiling killers, seen in those days as ridiculous as the paranormal events that Fox now devotes his energies to. The killer was one Harry Cokely, who carved the words 'brother' or 'sister' in the chests of his victims (depending on their sex),

was caught but is now released and an old man confined to his house. B. J. insists Harry is the killer after she wakes up to find 'sister' carved on her and sees a vision of the young Cokely in her room. Scully and Mulder bring him in but can pin nothing on him. B. J. finds another body, this time of Leadbetter after seeing more visions of the past, just as more murders bearing all the hallmarks of Cokely are committed. Scully interviews Mrs Thibodeaux, who survived Cokely's attack in the forties and finds out that she became pregnant as a result. Her and Cokely's son was put up for adoption — he is B. J.'s father. Morrow turns out to be the new murderer, having inherited all of Cokely's subconscious memories and impulses.

Comments:
A great story, where the sins of the father are visited not upon the son but the daughter. There is no real explantion for this one other than that B. J. is driven to kill by her genes, but how she knew where to find the old bodies is unclear — Mulder proposes that some specific memories can be passed from generation to generation, but the scientific explanation of encoded chemicals is pure speculation. Mulder mentions in passing that he is fascinated by women called BJ — this is a reference to Perrey Reeves, his then girlfriend, who was playing BJ on Doogie Howser at the time.

37: Irresistible
First Transmission 13th January 1995
Written by Chris Carter   Directed by David Nutter

Cast:
Bruce Weitz, Nick Chinlund, Deanna Milligan, Robert Thurston, Glynis Davies, Christine Willes, Tim Progosh, Dwight McFee, Denalda Williams, Maggie O'Hara, Kathleen Duborg, Mark Saunders, Ciara Hunter.

Story:
A Minnesota grave is desecrated and, thinking it the work of Aliens, Mulder and Scully are shipped in. The clues point to a human death fetishist, one whom Mulder believes will kill in the future. After a prostitute is killed by the same person, Scully finds a fingerprint which gives them the identity of Donnie Pfaster. She returns to the site but is kidnapped by Donnie and is about to be his next victim before Mulder and FBI agent Mo Blocks find and save her.

Comments:
A chilling episode and probably the only mainstream show on US TV to hint at necrophilia (this was more obvious in the original script but was toned down to fetishism when the studio expressed reservations). The visions Scully sees, where Pfaster changes form, are merely her disturbed mind at work rather than any alien or demonic prescence. An abbreviation of Scully and Mulder is S&M but that's just a coincidence, isn't it?

38: Die Hand die Verletzt
First Transmission 27th January 1995
Written by Morgan & Wong   Directed by Kim Manners

Cast:
Dan Butler, Susan Blommaert, Heather McComb, Shaun Johnston, P. Lynn Johnson, Travis MacDonald, Michell Godger, Larry E. Musser, Franky Czinege, Laura Harris, Doug Abrahams.

Story:
Milford, New Hampshire — that well-known cesspit of Satanism and Witchcraft — is the destination of the FBI's least-wanted this week, as Fox and Dana look into the case of a teenager killed by demonic forces. After some curious happenings Shannon Ausbury, a friend of the dead boy, apparently commits suicide after claiming she was ritually abused when young. The investigation flows from Shannon's father Jim to the sinister Mrs Paddock, a teacher who has appeared from nowhere. Jim is killed by a huge snake while Mulder and Scully are captured by the Satanic schoolteachers. They are only saved from ritual sacrifice by the intervention of Mrs Paddock, who vanishes without trace.

Comments:
The title is German for "The Hand, The Pain" which must be an allusion to Paddock's hand-burning activities to gain control of her victims. She is some sort of Emissary from a higher dark power sent to punish the local coven for their lack of faith, whose quarrel is not with the FBI.

39: Fresh Bones
First Transmission 3rd February 1995
Written by Howard Gordon Directed by Rob Bowman

Cast:
Bruce Young, Daniel Benzali, Jamil Walker Smith, Matt Hill, Callum Keith Rennie, Kevin Conway, Katya Gardner, Roger Cross, Peter Kelamis.

Story:
The second suicide in a month at an immigration processing centre in North Carolina attracts the attention of the FBI. The widow of Private McAlpin is adamant that her husband would never have committed suicide. A voodoo symbol found at the scene of death takes the investigation to Bauvais, the leader of the Haitian immigrants. Meanwhile, McAlpin's body is replaced by that of a dog and the dead soldier is found alive in the camp, having murdered his friend Harry Dunham. The culprit is Colonel Wharton, the camp commander, who is a voodoo practitioner having gone native once in Haiti, where he lost some men to the locals and is now taking revenge on them. Bauvais, killed by the Colonel, is resurrectd by voodoo and extracts a grisly revenge on Wharton.

Comments:
X appears again, though his and the conspiracy's involvements in this case is unclear. He contacts Mulder with the playing card the ten of diamonds, a coded reference to County Road 10. The poison used by the Colonel induces the zombie-like state, which explains the 'deaths' but some real voodoo is obviously at work here. A nice little chiller of an episode.

40: Colony
First Transmission 10th February 1995
Written by Chris Carter (story by Duchovny/Carter)
Directed by Nick Marck

Cast:
Dana Gladstone, Megan Leitch, Tom Butler, Tim Henry, Andrew Johnston, Ken Roberts, Michael Rogers, Oliver Becker, James Leard, Linden Banks, Bonnie Hay, Kim Restell, Richard Sargent, David L. Gordon.

Story:
Mulder and Scully look into a spate of arson attacks on abortion clinics that have killed three doctors, who turn out to be identical despite being unrelated. They look for other clones and find one, but cannot prevent him being killed either. Skinner takes the two out of active duty but, acting on a CIA tip-off that the clones are the result of a Cold-War experiment

being terminated by a Russian agent, they continue their work. Mulder is forced to return home where he finds his abducted sister Samantha has returned — she tells him that the assassin is a shapeshifting Alien. Scully finds the remaining clones but cannot prevent them being executed by the assassin and is taken prisoner by him, having assumed Mulders' form.

Comments:
The blood of the shapeshifter is still the lethal ooze as seen in 'The Erlenmyer Flask'. The true story is revealed next episode. The fake Mulder arrives at Scully's place at 11:21 and the name Ambrose Chapel comes from Hitchcock movie 'The Man Who Knew Too Much', where the name of a place is wrongly taken to be the name of a person — the same mistake made by Mulder and Scully.

41: End Game
First Transmission 17th February 1995
Written by Frank Spotnitz   Directed by Rob Bowman

Cast:
Megan Leitch, Colin Cunningham, Garry Davey, Andrew Johnston, Allan Lysell, J. B. Bivens, Oliver Becker, Beatrice Zeilinger, Bonnie Hay.

Story:
The story continues with Scully being held hostage by the assassin, who is after 'Samantha' at the Mulder residence. Skinner sets up an exchange, planning to shoot the Alien during the handover. The operation fails and both the Alien and Samantha disappear over the bridge they were on. Fox returns home where his father gives him a note from her, sending him to an abortion clinic in Rockville. While Scully is seeing one Samantha recovered from the river bed, Mulder is meeting a host of 'Samanthas' in the clinic. Mulder proves totally useless against the being we know now as the Pilot and they too are all killed. He tracks the Alien to the Arctic, where he succumbs to the Alien blood and is left alone on the freezing iceberg. He is saved by a rescue team, enabling Scully to use her experience of the toxic blood to save him.

Comments:
Take a deep breath — here goes: The shapeshifter race is the one which came to Earth in the 1940's and theirs is the DNA held by the US government, found in the Erlenmyer flask and other places. Their foetuses are as the ones held by Scully before Deep Throat's death. They established a colony of clones based on the original Doctor and Samantha and because of their looks had to scatter to avoid suspicion. The DNA experimentation must have been to find a way of producing non-identical clones, but the work of the Colony has since parted from the ideal held by the leaders of the Shapeshifter race (they are very keen on racial purity) and so have been eradicated by the shapeshifter/Human conspiracy. The conspiracy did take Samantha, so the stick-man Grey seen by Mulder as he remembers her abduction in 'Little Green Men' is either a decoy (pretty pointless as Bill Mulder knew the whole story and kiddie Fox would have been asleep) or the Greys are the Shapeshifters. Or Mulder is just making it up as he goes along. The toxic blood of the Aliens contains a retrovirus that triggers an immunological response, killing the infected person. It is dormant, like other viruses, at low temperatures and can be dealt with. These two episodes go a long way to explaining the entire conspiracy story of the X-Files. Scully receives an E-mail which reads "To: Dana Scully, 001013". Happy birthday, Chris!

42: Fearful Symmetry
First Transmission 24th February 1995

Written by Steve de Jarnatt   Directed by James Whitmore Jnr

Cast:
Jayne Atkinson, Lance Guest, Jack Rader, Jody St Michael, Charles Andre, Garvin Cross, Tom Glass.

Story:
An impossible zoo breakout brings our favourite FBI special agents to Fairfield, Idaho, but no sign of the escaped elephant can be found — because it is invisible. Scully blames local eco-warriors the WAO and follows one of them to the zoo. He is killed by an invisible tiger and Mulder contacts the Lone Gunmen, who tell him that no animal at that zoo has ever gone full term with a pregnancy. An autopsy on the newly-visible elephant reveals it had been pregnant.

Comments:
It seems that the Greys, or whoever the invisible Aliens in 'Fallen Angel' are, have been taking animal embryos for their own purposes. Why the parents then become invisible can only be assumed to be the effects of the Aliens work on them. Why they can't then put the animals back where they found them shows the Aliens have no respect for the Human way of doing things. No surprises there. They might be working on a project to save the animals of the Earth. Either way, their technology separates them from the shapeshifters, who cannot do invisibility or warp time (Mulder loses some more time here in a whiteout).

43: Død Kalm
First Transmission 10th March 1995
Written by Gordon & Gansa   Directed by Rob Bowman

Cast:
John Savage, David Cubitt, Vladimir Kulich, Stephen Dimopoulos, Claire Riley, Robert Metcalfe, Dmitri Chepovetsky.

Story:
The lone survivor of the USS Arden turns up, prematurely aged. Mulder and Scully charter a ship to the Arden's last location and find her remains, only to become stranded there. They find another prematurely aged man who dies and a pirate whaler who is unaffected. They discover that the water is to blame and the only safe supply is the rapidly-diminishing supply of recycled sewage water. They all begin to age but are rescued and recover their youth.

Comments:
There is mention here of the real-life Philadelphia experiment, which attempted to make ships invisible to radar. They succeeded using Alien technology found at Roswell and made a ship move through time and space. None of which is relevant to the story, which throws some pseudo-scientific guff about free-radicals, magnetic meteorites, wormholes and heavy salt

into an indistinguishable, unanswerable mess. Avoid like the plague.....

44: Humbug
First Transmission 31st March 1995
Written by Darin Morgan Directed by Kim Manners

Cast:
Jim Rose, Wayne Grace, Michael Anderson, The Enigma, Vincent Schiavelli, Alex Diakun, John Payne, Gordon Tipple, Alvin Law.

Story:
Gibsontown, Florida, is where all the circus freaks go to when they retire. 'Alligator Man' is killed in his home and the FBI is called in. Mulder and Scully find an assortment of oddballs and a multitude of suspects, including Sheriff Hamilton - formerly Jim-Jim the Dog-Faced Boy and Dr Blockhead, whose blood was found at the scene of the crime. The murderer is in fact a deformed siamese twin, capable of detaching himself from his able-bodied 'brother'. Over twenty-eight years, he has committed forty-eight such killings in a misguided attempt to find a new sibling. His latest try is also his last, when he encounters the jigsaw-tattooed man, reknowned for his ability to eat anything. Including deformed siamese twins.....

Comments:
Who needs actors when there is such a wealth of talent amongst all these real-life carnival people? Those tattoos are all genuine and 'The Enigma' really can eat anything. A gem of an episode which is funny, scary and has a proper ending. God bless Darin Morgan.

45: The Calusari
First Transmission 14th April 1995
Written by Sara B. Charno Directed by Michael Vejar

Cast:
Helene Clarkson, Joel Palmer, Lilyan Chauvin, Kay E. Kuter, Ric Reid, Christine Willes, Bill Dow, Jacqueline Dandeneau, Bill Croft, Campbell Lane, George Josef.

Two-year-old Teddy Holvey is killed in a fairground accident and a photograph of the scene, moments before, shows him following a balloon flying against the wind. Analysis of the picture shows a ghostly imprint of a child pulling the balloon. Scully suspects Golda, the childs' Romanian grandmother who is overly protective of the older brother, Charlie. Mr Holvey is soon killed in a freak garage-door accident and Golda dies performing a Romanian ritual. Charlie blames Michael, his stillborn brother. The ghost of Michael takes on Charlie's form and is taken in by Mrs Holvey, who tries to perform the same ritual Golda did. Michael turns violent and uses his powers to throw his mother and Scully about, but they are saved by the Calusari, a group of Romanian religious elders who exorcise him.

Comments:
A scary yet empty episode. Yet another mischievous spirit takes revenge on the living in a take on Omen II and The Exorcist, beaten only by a Rabbinical hit squad who pop in at the end (thank, err, God for that!).

46: F. Emasculata
First Transmission 28th April 1995
Written by Carter & Howard Gordon Directed by Rob Bowman

Cast:

Charles Martin Smith, Dean Norris, John Pyper-Ferguson, Angelo Vacco, Morris Panych, Lynda Boyd, John Tench, Alvin Sanders, Kim Kondrashoff, Chilton Crane, Bill Rowat, Jude Zachary.

Story:
Skinner sends the tremendous twosome to help local police catch a couple of escaped convicts. They soon find things are not what they seem, when the prison is quarantined and a dead inmate is taken away by men in biohazard suits. The infectious disease on the loose is the result of a failed experiment by a pharmaceutical company and the government is trying to cover it up. The remaining prisoner is found but is shot before Mulder can get any answers.

Comments:
CSM is here and so is the rest of the conspiracy, trying to cover up the experiments. As discovered later in 'Apocrypha', this is part of the conspiracy's plan to produce a hardier strain of human. Haemorrhagic fever is actually the symptom of tropical viral diseases like Ebola which tend not to spread because, victims of their own success, the subject is killed before it can be passed on. The F. Emasculata of the title is a beetle whose larvae carry the virus, which would explain it's infectious nature. The package received by the prisoner is number DDP112148. Happy birthday, Mrs Carter!

47: Soft Light
First Transmission 5th May 1995
Written by Vince Gilligan Directed by James Contner

Cast:
Tony Shalhoub, Kate Twa, Kevin McNulty, Nathaniel Deveaux, Robert Rozen, Donna Yamamoto, Forbes Angus, Guyle Frazier, Steve Bacic, Craig Brunanski.

Story:
A man has disappeared from his Virginia hotel room leaving only a shadow-like stain, so Detective Kelly Ryan, an old friend of Scully's, calls in the X-team. They follow the clues to Polarity Magnetics, a research lab, where Dr Chris Davey tells them of his partner, Dr Chester Banton, who was caught in a freak particle accident and has not been seen since. They find Banton who explains that his shadow has mutated into some sort of black hole or dark matter, which kills all who come into contact with it. They lose him and Mulder calls in X. Another death at the lab implies Banton kills himself, but it is Davey who died. Banton is now in the hands of X.

Comments:
X does his bit for the conspiracy (or possibly the CIA - either of whom would be very interested in such a weapon). Banton feared a brain-draining device which indicates conspiracy technology. Scully gives such a woeful description of dark matter one wonders how challenging her degree was..... A mini black hole as suggested would not only pull in it's victims but you as well, the surrounding room and eventually the whole world (err, obviously). There are many theories on what might constitute dark matter doing the rounds at the moment, but none of them would even come close to having the effect of reducing people to scorch marks. But hey, who wants realism?

48: Our Town
First Transmission 12th May 1995
Written by Frank Spotnitz Directed by Rob Bowman

Cast:
Caroline Kava, John Milford, Gary Grubbs, Timothy

Webber, John MacLaren, Robin Mossley, Gabrielle Miller, Hrothgar Matthews, Robert Moloney, Carrie Cain Sparks.

Story:
An inspector of the Chaco Chicken plant in Dudley, Arkansas, disappears when he is about to recommend it's closure on health and safety grounds. Scully and

Mulder cannot find anything but when a psychotic young woman is shot, they find she is supposed to be forty-seven years old and is suffering from Creutzfeldt-Jacob disease. The river is dredged and skeletons going back years are found, along with evidence of a cannibalistic cult. Scully is almost eaten by them but is saved at the last minute by Mulder.

Comments:
Walter Chaco lived with the cannibals in New Guinea in 1944 and brought back the idea to Arkansas, where it was embraced by the townspeople because of it's anti-ageing properties. The CJD appears to have come from the meat of Kearns, the eaten inspector. But CJD takes years to develop. Chaco Chicken may well be inspired by Choky Chicken, found in the cartoon 'Rocko's Modern Life'.

49: Anasazi
First Transmission 19th May 1995
Written by Chris Carter (from a story by Duchovny and Carter)
Directed by R. W. Goodwin

Cast:
Floyd Westerman, Michael David Simms, Renae Morriseau, Ken Camroux, Dakota House, Bernie Coulson, Mitchell Davies, Paul McLean.

Story:
A contact of the Lone Gunmen, a hacker known as the Thinker, has gained access to government files which detail the Alien prescence on Earth from the 1940s, but they are encoded in Navajo. Meanwhile, Mulder is behaving increasingly strangely and attacks Skinner. CSM talks with Bill Mulder, who then calls to Fox to see him but Bill is shot before Mulder can get to him. In an attempt to set Mulder's record straight, Scully takes away his gun for analysis but this leaves him defenceless when the Assassin — Krycek — comes for him. Mulder turns the tables and is about to kill Alex when Scully stops him the only way she can — she shoots Fox. She discovers Mulder's water is being infected with drugs to make him psychotic and takes him to recover in New Mexico. There they find a Navajo, Albert Hosteen, who can translate the files. The Navajo people show Mulder an old boxcar buried in the desert, recently uncovered by an earthquake, which Fox discovers is full of what look like Alien corpses. CSM is hot on his trail and has the boxcar burned with Mulder inside.

Comments:
The conspiracy is revealed to be truly international in scope and to involve Mulder's family. CSM says he did not sanction Bill Mulder's murder and given Krycek's state of mind this may be true. The beings found in the boxcar may be one of three things: real Aliens, Alien/Human hybrids or mutated Humans; what exactly they are remains in doubt. The Aliens who have been visiting the Anasazi tribe are assumed to be the Greys and are seemingly benign. They are the enemy of the conspiracy, who may be producing mutants who look like the Greys for unknown reasons. The people doing this for the conspiracy are Axis scientists who changed sides at the end of the war. A nice little cliffhanger too for the next season and a fast-paced episode with a strong story.

SEASON THREE

Executive Producer: Chris Carter
Co-Executive Producers: Howard Gordon, R. W. Goodwin
Supervising Producer: Charles Grant Craig
Producers: Joseph Patrick Finn, Kim Manners, Rob Bowman
Co-Producer: Paul Rabwin
Additional Cast: Ernie Foort (FBI Gate Guard), Lenno Britos (Louis Cardinal), John Neville (Well- Manicured Man), Don S. Williams (Elder), Jaap Broeker (The Stupendous Yappi), Brendan Beiser (Pendrell), Tyler Labine (Stoner), Nicole Parker (Chick).

50: The Blessing Way
First Transmission 22nd September 1995
Written by Chris Carter   Directed by R. W. Goodwin

Cast:
Floyd Westerman, Alf Humphreys, Dakota House, Michael David Simms, Forbes Angus, Mitch Davies, Benita Ha, Ian Victor.

Story:
Scully is cornered, loses her copy (and backup) of the translated MJ files and is suspended. CSM reports to the conspiracy that Mulder is dead and the information is safe. He is in fact alive and well and being looked after by the Anasazi, who put him through a healing ceremony where he undergoes a mystical near-death experience, talking to his dead father and Deep Throat. Scully discovers she has an implant and undergoes hypnotherapy to see how it got there, but it is unsuccessful. She goes to Bill Mulder's funeral where she is warned by the Well-Manicured Man that her life is in danger. She tries to prevent her sister Melissa from going to her apartment but is held up by Skinner and Melissa is shot by Krycek. Scully and Skinner end the episode holding each other at gunpoint.

Comments:
The conspiracy comprises of the Well-Manicured Man, the Elder and at least six others who meet together physically in the USA on a regular basis. Along with CSM they represent a group of international world concerns which transcends the governments, although as this episode proves they cannot control federal judges. Their two methods of having you killed are (1) Human hitmen who will shoot you with an unregistered weapon, or (2) someone you trust coming to do the deed, which is probably a reference to a shapeshifter assassin. Some interesting revelations, but did we all have to sit through Deep Throat's meaningless babble on the afterlife?

51: Paper Clip
First Transmission 29th September 1995
Written by Chris Carter   Directed by Rob Bowman

Cast:
Walter Gotell, Floyd Westerman, Robert Lewis.

Story:
Mulder stops Scully and Skinner from shooting each other and Skinner reveals he has the missing back-up of the MJ files. Mulder has a photograph of his father with the conspirators which he shows to the Gunmen; they tell him that one of the men is Victor Klemper, a war criminal now living in America. Fox and Dana visit him and he guides them to a disused mine before informing the conspiracy that Mulder is still alive. Skinner goes back to see Melissa in hospital but is accosted by Krycek and his goons and loses the tape – but CSM has other ideas and, in an attempt to curry favour with the conspiracy who have disapproved of his violent methods, goes all caring and pacifist and orders Krycek blown up with a car bomb. Alex survives and makes off with the tape. Mulder and Scully arrive at the mine and find an enormous store for the records that the conspiracy has taken, which includes Scully, Samantha and tissue samples of each of the thousands of abducted people. They are split up and while Mulder witnesses a huge spaceship flying overhead, Scully finds a group of hybrids/mutants. The foot soldiers of the conspiracy arrive but Mulder and Scully escape. Skinner has arranged it so that they are free: the contents of the tape have been learnt by the Anasazi. Melissa dies in hospital.

Comments:
We learn that Bill Mulder worked for the State Department (whatever that means) and his work, gathering data on the American population in the event of a nuclear attack, was used to choose who should be abducted and used in the Alien hybrid experiments. The Roswell crash in 1947 was the source of the Alien DNA. Since then the shapeshifters have come on the scene and although they seem to have given some samples of their own DNA to the conspiracy, their aim is to stop this being used. They don't mind the Grey/Human hybrids, the ones Scully encounters in the mine, although why the conspiracy wants to make them is a mystery. The Greys are probably trying to save these mutants by taking them from the mine and it is their ship which Mulder sees.

52: D. P. O.
First Transmission 6th October 1995
Written by Howard Gordon   Directed by Kim Manners

Cast:
Giovanni Ribisi, Jack Black, Ernie Lively, Karen Witter, Steve Makaj, Peter Anderson, Kate Robbins, Mar Andersons, Brent Chapman, Jason Anthony Griffith.

Story:
Darren Peter Oswald survives a lightning strike and has been near the scene of numerous such strikes in the area. He attracts the suspicion of Mulder and Scully when they see him apparently stop and restart his boss' heart, but is released by a skeptical sheriff. Oswald goes beserk and kills his best friend before kidnapping a teacher, but is caught and struck by lightning again. He survives and is arrested, but

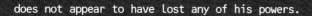

does not appear to have lost any of his powers.

Comments:
After the hectic conspiracy schedule it's back to creepy outsiders with paranormal powers, this time the ability to manipulate electrical fields. A cunning little episode showing the disenfranchised youth most likely to watch the show, in the worst light possible. Carter's name is shown near the end on a television that Oswald is watching.

53: Clyde Bruckman's Final Repose
First Transmission 13th October 1995
Written by Darin Morgan   Directed by David Nutter

Cast:
Peter Boyle, Stu Charno, Frank Cassini, Dwight McFee, Alex Diakun, Karin Konoval, Ken Roberts, David Mackay, Greg Anderson.

Story:
A serial killer has decided to start bumping off psychics, so naturally the Stupendous Yappi, a fake of the highest order, is called in to see what he can find. Mulder is overtly skeptical but they soon find a genuine fortune teller, Mr Bruckman. He is an insurance salesman who has just found another body and has the ability to see how people will die. Clyde forsees Mulder's murder and that Scully will hold his hand in bed. The killer comes to kill Bruckman but Mulder gives chase and, thanks to the warning given by Clyde, defeats him. Bruckman, no longer able to cope with his ability, takes an overdose and dies, Scully holding his hand.

Comments:
Uri Geller really should sue, as Yappi not only looks but sounds like him. Once again, Darin Morgan produces a wonderful comedy that remains faithful to the core of the X-Files. Scully gets a dog from this episode (bad news for the dog – see 'Quagmire') and learns that she doesn't die. One of Darin's in-jokes or a story thread to be picked up in the future? Clyde's lottery numbers were 9, 13, 37, 39, 41 and 45 – each digit one higher than the winning numbers. Pray that you can change the future.....

54: The List
First Transmission 20th October 1995
Written by Chris Carter   Directed by Chris Carter

Cast:
Bokeem Woodbine, Badja Djola, John Toles-Bey, Ken Foree, April Grace, J. T. Walsh, Greg Rogers, Mitchell Kosterman, Paul Raskin, Denny Arnold, Craig Brunanski, Joseph Patrick Finn.

Story:
Napoleon 'Neech' Manley goes to the chair protesting his innocence and swearing revenge on those he saw as framing him. Fox and Dana arrive after a prison guard is killed and find that Neech made a list of five people he was going to kill, each of whom start dying in impossible circumstances. The dynamic duo are powerless to prevent the prison governor and the new lover of Neech's widow being killed.

Comments:
Scully mentions her strict Catholic upbringing and producer Joseph Patrick Finn makes an appearance as the chaplain. Which doesn't stop this from being a dull, plodding episode.

55: 2Shy
First Transmission 3rd November 1995
Written by Jeffrey Vlaming   Directed by David Nutter

Cast:
Timothy Carhart, Catherine Paolone, James Handy, Kerry Sandomirsky, Aloka Mclean, Suzy Joachim, Glynis Davies, Randi Lynne, William MacDonald.

Story:
A woman on a blind date is killed and covered in slime, having lost lots of fatty tissue. Mulder sets about chasing a suspect from similar killings but their break comes when he kills again and they find that the victim met her murderer through the internet. They deduce his identity from the messages he gave her and find his files, leading them to his next intended victim. Scully stays by her and captures the man.

Comments:
The killer, Virgil Encanto, is another mutant along the lines of Tooms, but only possesses the ability to charm women via poetry over the internet (not an inconsiderable talent actually). Mulder tells Scully about the test results at 10:13. Happy birthday, Chris!

56: The Walk
First Transmission 10th November 1995
Written by John Shiban   Directed by Rob Bowman

Cast:
Thomas Kopache, Willie Garson, Don Thompson, Nancy Sorel, Iab Tracey, Pula Shaw, Deryl Hayes, Rob Lee, Andrea Barclay, Beatrice Zeilinger.

Story:
Suicide attempt rates at an army veterans' hospital are reaching epidemic proportions when Mulder and Scully are called in, whose investigation is stymied by General Callahan. Quinton Freely, a nurse, is arrested as he delivered mail to all the victims' homes, but he is working for Leonard Trimble, a quadruple amputee who needed the letters to form a psychic link with the victims, which he killed remotely. Quinton is suffocated and Trimble uses his power to kill the General's family. Callahan then goes to kill Leonard but, realising this is what he wants, lets him live. A former victim of Trimble chokes him with a pillow.

Comments:
Trimble's pscyhokinetic abilities are a result of his 'phantom limbs', with which he can stalk the Earth and make sure his fellow soldiers have to suffer with him. A nice criticism of the coverage of the Gulf War and a thought-provoking episode all round.

57: Oubliette
First Transmission 17th November 1995
Written by Charles Grant Craig Directed by Kim Manners

Cast:
Tracey Ellis, Michael Chieffo, Jewel Staite, Ken Ryan, Dean Wray, Jaques LaLonde, David Fredericks,

Sidonie Boll, Robert Underwood, Dolly Scarr, Bonnie Hay, David Lewis.

Story:
A little girl, Amy Jacobs, is kidnapped and Lucy Householder, who was held for five years by the same man seems to know all about it — even having a nose-bleed which turns out to be Amy's blood group and not hers. Following Lucy's lead they find the kidnapper, Karl Wade, but are too late. They discover the oubliette in his house where Lucy was kept all those years but Lucy's link leads them to the river, where Wade is in the process of drowning her. She stays under too long to survive but Lucy drowns in her place.

Comments:
There is no explanation other than Lucy having some sort of psychic link which goes beyond the traditional boundaries of space. Mulder now shoots first and asks questions later.

58: Nisei
First Transmission 24th November 1995
Written by Carter, Gordon & Spotnitz
Directed by David Nutter

Cast:
Stephen McHatie, Robert Ito, Gillian Barber, Corrine Koslo, Lori Triolo, Paul McLean, Yasuo Sakura.

Story:
A video of what looks like an Alien autopsy being carried out by Japanese scientists comes to Mulder's attention. He discovers the supplier murdered by a Japanese diplomat he finds on the scene. The man is freed but Mulder has secured his briefcase, which contains photographs that the Gunmen identify as satellite pictures of a ship and a list of local members of MUFON, a UFO society. Scully accidentally finds a house full of women who are a mutually-supportive UFO abductee group and learns that like them, she will eventually develop cancer. She also has the implant analysed — it is a very advanced computer chip — and remembers some more about her experience. Mulder goes on his own to find the ship and discovers what looks like a UFO in a nearby hangar. He learns the Japanese diplomat has been killed and goes to Senator Matheson who advises him to return the stolen information. He finds a train car carrying what looks like a live Alien and boards it.

Comments:
Dr Ishimaru was a member of the Japanese medical corps unit 731 who experimented on troops during the war. He came to the USA as part of operation Paper Clip and is a principle member of the abduction team that took Scully. It's a bit of a shocker to find that it was Humans who took Scully (and pretty much everybody else who says they were abducted).

59: 731
First Transmission 1st December 1995
Written by Frank Spotnitz Directed by Rob Bowman

Cast:
Stephen McHattie, Michael Puttonen, Robert Ito, Colin Cunningham.

Story:
Scully follows the trail of her implant to a Dr Zama at an institute in West Virginia, a camp for deformed Humans he experimented on. These people have just been killed and buried in a mass grave by soldiers but an identically-mutated being is on the boxcar that Mulder is now on. He finds and fights an NSA man who was there to stop Zama (who is actually Ishimaru) taking it out of the country — he also reveals that there is a bomb on board. Scully follows her own leads and finds the Elder, who informs her that the people in the institute were leper victims (Hansen's Disease) and other impoverished minorities who were used for disease and radiation experiments. Dana uses what she has found to work out the exit codes for the boxcar that Fox is now locked in, but he is surprised by the NSA man and left to die in the explosion with the mutant/hybrid. X arrives, shoots the NSA agent and carries away the unconscious Mulder, taking Ishimaru's real journals with him.

Comments:
The mystery deepens. If they aren't Alien hybrids in the train or in the mass grave, then they must be Humans used by the conspiracy or the government (or both) in an ongoing attempt to create a disease and radiation-proof Human that can be used for military purposes. If they are hybrids then that would explain their killings — racial purity must be maintained by the conspiracy. Or it could just be the government covering up their past transgressions and dabblings in eugenics. Any of the factions would be interested in making a super-soldier (and would be willing to kill to ensure no other country got hold of one), so either explanation is possible — but what about that Alien craft in the hangar last week? Is the creature in the boxcar a real hybrid? A real Alien? Either way, the green blood seen in the video implies toxic shapeshifter blood. The boxcar combination is 101331. Happy birthday, Chris!

60: Revelations
First Transmission 15th December 1995
Written by Kim Newton Directed by David Nutter

Cast:
Kevin Zegers, Sam Bottoms, Kenneth Welsh, Michael Berryman, Hayley Tyson, R. Lee Ermey, Lesly Ewen, Fulvio Cecere, Nicole Robert.

Story:
A serial killer has so far murdered eleven fake stigmatics and the next target, a boy called Kevin who is a real stigmatic, is kidnapped. He is found by Mulder and Scully but the kidnapper, Jarvis, is killed by the real murderer, a businessman called Simon Gates. Gates has hands which can burn, a power he developed on returning from Jerusalem. He takes Kevin from under the noses of Fox and Dana and takes him to be killed at a recycling plant. Scully goes there and saves Kevin.

Comments:
Real 'Omen' stuff here as the forces of good and evil battle against one another. Kevin's ability to be in more than one place at the same time is quite extraordinary. If he really is the second coming, you'd have thought God would have chosen a better name for his representative on Earth than "Kevin".....

61: War of the Coprophages
First Transmission 5th January 1996

Written by Darin Morgan Directed by Kim Manners

Cast:
Bobbie Phillilps, Raye Birk, Dion Anderson, Bill Dow, Alex Bruhanski, Ken Kramer, Alan Buckley, Maria Herrera, Sean Allan, Norma Wick, Wren Robertz, Tom Heaton, Bobby L. Stewart, Dawn Stofer, Fiona Roeske.

Story:
Multiple deaths seemingly caused by cockroaches with ultra-hard exoskeletons take Mulder to the Department of Agriculture, where he finds a house built especially for cockroaches. Working there is Bambi, an entomologist who helps him look in to the problem. He visits Dr Ivanov, an expert on advanced robotics, who hypothesises that the metallic insects may be robot probes gathering information. Scully flies in to find the town in a state of panic, the population of which think an infestation is coming that will bring disease. After a chat with the doctor, Mulder goes to the local methane plant (every town should have one) on the basis that they might be 'refuelling' there. The owner is an insectophobe and goes crazy, blowing up the plant and with it any trace of the killer bugs. Bambi and the doctor go off together into the sunset.

Comments:
Can Darin do no wrong? Not so far. A beautiful episode which brings in a whole new category of passive observer-Aliens that is bang-up-to-date with current thinking on space exploration. And a truly disgusting toilet scene. What more could you want? Yes, I know, but they couldn't possibly put that in an X-Files episode. News reporter Skye Leikin is named after a fan who won a contest to get his name on the show and Dr Bambi Berenbaum is named after Dr May R Berenbaum, Head of Entymology at the University of Illinois.

62: Syzygy
First Transmission 26th January 1996
Written by Chris Carter Directed by Rob Bowman

Cast:
Dana Wheeler-Nicholson, Wendy Benson, Lisa Robin Kelly, Garry Davey, Denalda Williams, Gabrielle Miller, Ryan Reynolds, Tim Dixon, Ryk Brown, Jeremy Radick, Russell Porter.

Story:
There's something witchy going on at Grover Cleveland Alexander High School, Comity, where three boys have been killed and the latest victim's coffin bursts into flames at the funeral. Two girls, Terri Roberts and Margi Kleinjan, were with him last and Mulder

takes his new paramour, Detective Angela White, to see an astrologer. The two witchlets kill another boy and bones are found in a local field, but they are those of a dog. Another girl is killed by Terri and Margi but they fall out over a boy and accidentally kill him too, accusing each other of the crime. The townsfolk form a lynching mob to get the girls at the police station. As they use their demonic powers against each other midnight passes, and with it their supernatural abilities.

Comments:
The rather pathetic excuse for this plot is some astrological conjunction of the planets. Any story would have done to see Mulder and Scully acting against character with Fox knocking back vodka and hangin wit' his wumman while Scully smokes and bitches away. Mulder brings in one of the girls at 11:48. Happy birthday, Mrs Carter!

63: Grotesque
First Transmission 2nd February 1996
Written by Howard Gordon Directed by Kim Manners

Cast:
Levani, Kurtwood Smith, Greg Thirloway, Susan Bain, Kasper Michaels, Zoran Vukelic.

Story:
A serial killer is caught and claims he was possessed by a spirit, which seems to be true as while he is in custody another murder is committed. Bill

Patterson, the senior FBI man on the case, resents Mulder's involvement, especially when he finds the killer's lair where the victims are encased in clay gargoyles. Mulder gets inside the killers' head a little too well and decorates his room with gargoyle drawings, sleeping in the murderer's bed where he is attacked by a man wearing a gargoyle mask. Patterson's assistant is killed and it turns out Bill is the killer, driven mad by his years of studying the darkest depths of Human nature.

Comments:
Mulder sure knows how to pick his friends. It's good to see Fox doing some proper FBI work again and seeing how good he is supposed to be. Agent Nemhauser gets his name from the post-production supervisor, Lori Jo Nemhauser. Psychology students love this one.

64: Piper Maru
First Transmission 9th February 1996
Written by Carter & Spotnitz Directed by Rob Bowman

Cast:
Robert Clothier, Jo Bates, Morris Fanych, Stephen E. Miller, Ari Solomon, Paul Batten, Russell Ferrier, Kimberly Unger, Rochelle Greenwood, Joel Silverstone, David Neale, Tom Scholte, Robert F. Maier.

Story:
An aeroplane on the ocean floor is salvaged by a French ship, but a diver sent down to investigate is possessed by Alien slime which finishes off the rest of the crew with radiation. While Scully speaks to an old friend of her father's (who tells of a submarine mission to recover a lost B-52 carrying a nuclear weapon many years ago), Mulder follows up the trail of the craft he saw in 'Nisei' and finds Krycek in Hong Kong. Alex and his salvage partner Jerry have been selling the MJ files' secrets for a tidy profit up until now. The slime meanwhile has been transferred to the divers' wife, who follows Fox to Hong Kong and takes out a group of French agents with more radiation bursts. Skinner is shot by US agents and the Slime possesses Krycek.

Comments:
The story given to Scully is a lie and covers up the truth of a real operation to recover a downed UFO by the US – which ended in disaster as the captain was taken by the ooze. Scully seems to have an encyclopaedic knowledge of aeroplanes thanks to watching a few models being built by her childhood friends. Skinner is threatened by men who could be from anyone, seeing as how he's annoyed just about everyone from the conspiracy elders to the county sheriff's office. The Alien slime is...EITHER an entirely new race (unlikely), the 'real' form of the shapeshifters (equally unlikely, unless it's a rebel) or another form of the Greys (possible, since it's principle weapon is radiation, which the conspiracy is interested in finding a defence against). Effects supervisor Dave Gaulthier gets his name in lights this episode and there's another celebration – Mulder's flight back to Washington is number 1121. Happy birthday, Mrs Carter!

65: Apocrypha
First Transmission 16th February
Written by Carter & Spotnitz Directed by Kim Manners

Cast:
Kevin McNulty, Barry Levy, Dmitry Chepovetsky, Sue Mathew, Frances Flanagan, Peter Scoular, Jeff Chivers, Martin Evans.

Story:
Mulder and Krycek drive around Washington, hoping to retrieve the MJ files from the deposit-box they are kept in. Attacked by CSM's men, Krycek fights them off with a radiation burst. Scully follows the clues left by Skinner's assailant and discovers it was the same man who shot her sister – she demands that the FBI re-open the investigation and pursue Krycek. Fox brings in the Lone Gunmen to obtain the files, but the deposit-box is empty and Alex has disappeared. Mulder meets the Well-Manicured Man who tells him that Skinner is still on the hit-list, so Scully keeps watch on him and catches Louis Cardinal, the man who shot Melissa and tried to kill Skinner. Louis trades his life for the information that Krycek is making his way to a missile silo in Dakota, where the recovered UFO from WWII was moved to. Mulder and Scully get there but cannot get past CSM and his men. The Slime leaves Alex and seeps inside the spacecraft, leaving him entombed within the silo.

Comments:
No-one seems to know what exactly the slime is now, but it is an inhabitant of the triangular ship which is almost identical to the one seen in 'Deep Throat', which was obtained by the military in the forties after it was shot down (how bad can these Aliens be if they are scuppered by Iraqi pilots and WWII planes?). CSM, Bill Mulder and presumably Deep Throat were an investigative team at this time and CSM at least has seen the effects of the slime before, when it tried to take over the submarine but was thwarted. The craft was later recovered by the conspiracy and held in Nevada (presumably Area 51) but has recently been moved now everyone knows about the base there. The French agents seem to be involved because they want the Slime for their own use (perhaps for some experiments like the ones in 'Terma') or maybe they have been excluded by the conspiracy and are one of Krycek's buyers for the MJ Files. While on the sea bed, the slime got out of the triangular craft and took residence in the body of the pilot, presumably for just such an opportunity as the diver presented. However, since it has been down there for fifty years couldn't it have crawled along the ocean floor itself, or possessed a fish and started swimming? The conspiracy met at 46th Street, New York and their telephone number is 5551012. Carter was obviously so miffed that a typing mistake robbed him of another personal treat that the missile silo was hastily re-numbered 1013. Happy birthday, Chris!

66: Pusher
First Transmission 23rd February 1996
Written by Vince Gilligan Directed by Rob Bowman

Cast:
Robert Wisden, Vic Polizos, Roger R. Cross, Steve Bacic, Don Mackay, Brent Sheppard, D. Neil Mark, Meredith Bain Woodward, Julia Arkos, Darren Lucas.

Story:
A criminal has already confessed his part in several 'suicide' killings to Frank Burst, a detective who calls in Fox and Dana to help. They track the man calling himself 'The Pusher' to a golf course

where he makes a man set himself on fire and is caught. Mulder once more comes across as a mad hatter during testimony and this, coupled with The Pusher's influence on the judge means he is set free. The Pusher goes to the FBI offices and looks at private files, only pausing to make a secretary attack Skinner. Revealed to be a terminally-ill brain cancer sufferer, The Pusher has a showdown with Mulder, forcing him to play Russian Roulette and almost makes him shoot Scully. She breaks his concentration with the fire alarm and Fox shoots The Pusher.

Comments:
The Pusher is a little man whose fatal disease gives him the power to finally be somebody, an opportunity he grabs with both hands. What have the writers got against Skinner? He's been at the receiving end of more violence this season than anyone else and suffers the indignity of being bested by someone who looks like they just came in from college for work-experience. In the trash tabloid World Weekly Informer there are the headlines 'Flukeman Found Washed Up In Martha's Vineyard' and 'Depravity Rampant On Hit TV Show'. Dave Grohl of the Foo Fighters (an old Air Force designation for a UFO) and formerly Nirvana makes a cameo appearance with his wife as The Pusher goes into the FBI building.

67: Teso dos Bichos
First Transmission 8th March 1996
Written by John Shiban Directed by Kim Manners

Cast:
Vic Trevino, Janne Mortil, Gordon Tootoosis, Tom McBeath, Ron Suave, Alan Robertson, Garrison Chrisjohn.

Story:
At an Ecuadorian archaeological dig, the body of a female Shaman is dug up and sent to a museum in Boston, despite protests that it should remain where it was found. Academics at the museum start to vanish and suspicion falls on Belack, the curator's assistant, who spends an unhealthy amount of time consuming Ecuadorian herbal remedies. His friend Mona disappears soon after finding the toilets full of rats, so Fox and Dana chase Belack into the sewers where they find the missing bodies and a horde of killer cats. They escape and the Shaman's remains are returned to Ecuador.

Comments:
Another nasty ghost story, this time jazzed up with some South-American frills. Still a great episode though, with a high gore quotient and lots of deserving deaths. For a horde of blood-crazed animals who spend their time gorging on entrails and living in the sewers, those cats are damn clean. Dr Lewton is named after Val Newton, the producer of cult hit 'Cat People'.

68: Hell Money
First Transmission 29th March 1996
Written by Jeffrey Vlaming Directed by Tucker Gates

Cast:
B. D. Wong, Lucy Alexis Liu, James Hong, Michael Yama, Doug Abrahams, Ellie Harvie, Derek Lowe, Donald Fong, Diana Ha, Stephen M. D. Chang, Paul Wong.

Story:
A murdered man's body is found in a crematorium, along with a scrap of Hell Money - ceremonial notes, used to appease the dead in Chinese burials and Chinese characters are found on the door of the deceased's house. In San Francisco, a secret lottery is being held by the Chinese community where you could win everything or lose an organ and possibly your life. Mr Hsin, a local man, has already lost an eye to the organisation trying to pay for his daughter's operation and now loses big-time. Fortunately, Scully and Mulder have followed the trail of a rogue doctor to the lottery where they find their policeman friend, Chao. He was working for the lottery bosses but his conscience gets the better of him and he exposes it for a fix. Mr Hsin is saved but nobody will testify and the leaders go free. Chao is killed for his pains.

Comments:
A slice of real police drama that's more along the lines of Hill Street Blues or Homicide: Life On The Street, as our heroes stumble upon a horrendous wall of silence maintained by the very people who are terrorised and conned. They can do nothing but temporarily stop the operation and watch the bosses walk, while good guy Chao gets it in the neck. The 'ghosts' of the beginning don't seem to be anything more supernatural than a bunch of thugs in masks working for the lottery. The scariest thing about this episode is that it probably is happening somewhere.....

69: Jose Chung's 'From Outer Space'
First Transmission 12th April 1996
Written by Darin Morgan Directed by Rob Bowman

Cast:
Charles Nelson Reilly, William Lucking, Daniel Quinn, Jesse Ventura, Sarah Sawatsky, Jason Gaffney, Alex Diakun, Larry Musser, Alex Trebeck, Allan Zinyk, Andrew Turner, Michael Dobson, Mina E. Mina.

Story:
Scully spends some time with Jose Chung, a novellist who is interested in writing a book on the paranormal (Mulder refuses to speak with him). Fox interviews a pair of would-be abductees, a girl and a boy who tell different stories; she gives the standard abduction story while the boy talks of a cigarette-smoking Alien (!). A nearby telephone engineer saw the Aliens and was visited by Men in Black (not Will Smith and Tommy-Lee Jones unfortunately). The girl Mulder spoke to is hypnotised again and remembers USAF men instead, when what looks like a dead Alien is found - an autopsy reveals it is a USAF Major in a suit. Another pilot comes forward to speak to Mulder and tells him of Air Force secret craft being used to abduct citizens, the crew disguised as Aliens. Mulder and Scully are later met by the MiB, one of them looking like game-show host Alex Trebeck and another a dead-ringer for Jesse ("The Body") Ventura, an ex-WWF wrestler! Scully is later unable to recall this meeting. They are then shown a crash site of one of these secret aircraft, where the dead body of the pilot who spoke to Mulder lies. Mulder goes to Chung to stop him publishing, for fear that it will make everything look ridiculous but 'From Outer Space' goes out anyway.

Comments:
The USAF has been using these secret aircraft (based

on the 'Apocrypha' Alien design) to carry out a pro-gram of abductions. These hapless subjects then have their memory of the event wiped. The pilot explains to Mulder that this is to test new reconnaissance aircraft and the myth of Aliens and UFO's is put about to stop them getting shot at (obviously nobody told the Iraqis about this - or, come to think of it, any-body else, because it seems to be Air Force policy the world over to take pot-shots at UFO's whenever possible). The pilot says he and his partner were themselves abducted by 'Lord Kinbote' (a Japanese comic character) which appears to be a device used by shapeshifting Aliens to make witnesses accounts appear ridiculous (it works). They employ their tech-nology for memory-wiping (used by the conspiracy and the government as well) to make sure that two peo-ple have conflicting reports of the same event (like the boy and the girl who spoke to Mulder). Klass County is named after Philip J. Klass, a UFO skep-tic and surnames used by characters include Vallee, Schaffer and Hynek, all UFO experts. The show final-ly acknowledges that it's mythology has passed into the public consciousness and is deliberately self-referential here, as the investigation becomes a vic-tim of it's own success. Everybody knows what Aliens look like, don't they? We know what they do, right? How Mulder and Scully can take themselves seriously after this is beyond me. And it's nice to know that not only can encounters with the MiB lead to you win-ning tonight's mystery prize, but you can also be suplexed off the top-rope too! Note to non-Americans who are wondering who Alex Trebeck is: just imagine you're abducted and Jim Davidson appears to oversee your flight. Now go and have a nice lie down.....

70: Avatar
First Transmission 26th April 1996
Written by Howard Gordon, from a story by Duchovny & Gordon   Directed by James Charleston

Cast:
Tom Mason, Jennifer Hetrick, Amanda Tapping, Malcolm Stewart, Morris Panych, Michael David-Simms, Stacy Grant, Janie Woods-Morris.

Story:
Skinner wakes up next to a dead prostitute with no memory of what happened the night before and starts having visions of a strange old woman, who appar-ently saved him during his days in Vietnam. He is being treated for a sleep disorder and soon goes to see his injured wife, who has just been run off the road. Scully finds a phosphorescent substance on the dead woman's mouth and Fox discovers the imprint of a man's face on the passenger airbag of Skinner's wife's car. While Walter is being dismissed, Mulder and Scully find that the man whose face was on the airbag hired the prostitute, but cannot stop the madam being killed in a fall. They set a trap for the man but he spots it and Scully (wearing a bul-letproof vest) is shot. Skinner, returning from the bedside of his comatose wife, arrives to shoot the man but will not say what it was the mysterious old woman said to him at the hospital.

Comments:
Having failed to kill Skinner, the conspiracy seems to be trying to frame him and they do a damn good job of it too, almost discrediting Mulder and Scully in the process . The substance found on the girl's lip may be the memory-wiping chemical so beloved of the conspiracy. Jennifer Hetrick, Skinner's wife Sharon, also played Captain Picard's girlfriend in Star Trek: TNG. "Engage".....

71: Quagmire
First Transmission 3rd May
Written by Kim Newton Directed by Kim Manners

Cast:
Chris Ellis, Timothy Webber, R. Nelson Brown, Mark Acheson, Peter Hanlon, Terrance Leigh.

Story:
Heuvelman's Lake, Georgia, is the scene for some unexplained missing persons which draws the atten-tion of Fox and Dana with stories of a monster called 'Big Blue'. They talk to biologist Dr Faraday, who complains of a mass frog exodus from the lake and

then find a half-eaten body prompting the lake to be closed to the public. After Scully's dog is snatched from her by an unseen beast, the pair throw caution to the wind and row out on the lake only to be marooned on a rock. They turn out to be much closer to the shore than imagined and, on Mulder's insistence, hunt for the creature in the woods. He finds a giant alligator which is swiftly despatched and they leave, just in time to miss the real monster making an appearance.

Comments:
Call me Ishmael. All right, don't, but that won't stop this being a big Moby Dick rip-off, right down to the little dog called Queequeeg (a character from the book). Cap'n Mulder ploughs ahead in his obsessive cause to find the monster and of course fails heroically, killing a relatively normal beast (boo, hiss) which was actually responsible for the disappearances. Not that this matters, because this is another lovely, funny episode which doesn't have to rely on the Aliens for it's story.

72: Wetwired
First Transmission 10th May 1996
Written by Mat Beck   Directed by Rob Bowman

Cast:
Colin Cunningham, Tim Henry, Linden Banks, Crystal Verge, Andre Danyliu, Joe Maffei, John McConnach, Joe Do Serro, Heather McCarthy.

Story:
Mulder is contacted by an informant and told to look into a case of a mild-mannered man who went berserk and killed five people, thinking they were all a Serbian war criminal. Scully goes through the killers enormous tape collection of daytime television and finds mention of the war criminal sought by the murderer. That night she sees Mulder in a car, having a friendly conversation with CSM. More killings occur and Mulder follows a television engineer who is putting a gold device into cable TV boxes. The Lone Gunmen say it can be used to send images between the frames of a television picture. Scully becomes increasingly paranoid and nearly shoots Mulder before going missing. Mulder finds her at her mother's house, where she is persuaded not to kill him by Mrs Scully. Mulder goes to track down the doctor who examined the first killer having seen him in conversation with CSM, but before he can do so X bursts in and shoots everyone. X goes off to report to CSM that all is well.

Comments:
X tried to tie up the loose ends as slowly as he could, but Scully's actions forced his hand and he could not let Mulder go any further. This is obviously the conspiracy at work on more mind-control devices, but why they would knowingly put all this effort into a device which doesn't affect colour-blind people (like Mulder) when they make up a sizeable minority is anybody's guess. Oh well.....

73: Talitha Cumi
First Transmission 17th May 1996
Written by Chris Carter, from a story by Duchovny and Carter Directed by R. W. Goodwin

Cast:
Roy Thinnes, Angelo Vacco, Hrothgar Mathews, Stephen Demopoulos, John MacLaren, Cam Cronin, Bonnie Ray.

Story:
A mad gunman runs amok in a burger joint. A man calling himself Jeremiah Smith heals the victims and runs away. CSM visits Mrs Mulder and tries to get her to remember something and when he leaves, she suffers a stroke leaving Mulder the cryptic message 'palm' on a note. CSM finds Jeremiah and brings him in, while X shows Mulder what happened to his mother. Smith now turns himself into the FBI and answers their questions without telling them anything and the investigation is closed. Mulder goes to his mothers' beach house and realises that 'palm' is an anagram of 'lamp' and finds an Alien weapon hidden there. CSM goes to the FBI and interviews Smith again, where it is revealed Jeremiah is a rebel shapeshifter trying to give Humans hope. He cures CSM of his lung cancer and is freed. Mulder and Scully have been chasing Smith, but when they find him they discover they have been chasing the Pilot, sent to kill Smith. CSM visits Mrs Mulder in hospital and tells Fox that Smith knows what happened to Samantha. X later confronts Mulder and they fight over the Alien weapon before backing off. Jeremiah visits Scully and tells her of a plan that involves Samantha when Mulder arrives and demands Smith heal his mother. The Pilot arrives and tries to kill Smith.

Comments:
CSM and the Mulders go back a long way, from before the time Mulder was born. It is clearly implied the CSM and Mrs Mulder had an affair (and even that he may be Fox's father) which would explain his reactions to her stroke, but what could he have been trying to get her to remember from all those years back at the summer house in Quonochontaug? Could it be that she was abducted and Fox is the resulting product of CSM/Mrs Mulder/Alien DNA? How nice it would be to think so. The shapeshifting talent of healing is revealed, as Smith has the power to completely negate the effects of gunshot wounds and extensive cancers. Jeremiah is a junior conspiracy member who has lost all faith in the 'greater purpose' and now just wants to give Humans hope. Either he is a mindreader or he has foreknowledge of CSM's past life, as his transformations into Bill Mulder and Deep Throat show some insight into CSM's character (as well as providing a useful half day's work for the actors involved). CSM knows that only an Alien weapon in the back of the neck can kill a shapeshifter, so he sends for the Pilot to do the deed. A date is set for the colonisation of Earth and the shapeshifters need us to lose faith in everything but science to do this. CSM wants to be some kind of camp commandant when we are rounded up by the Aliens (and mutated?). The plan surrounding Samantha is common knowledge to both Alien sides, and may be completely separate from the colonisation project. We are so close to the truth this time....'Talitha Cumi' is classical Greek for 'little girl, get up', used by Jesus when he heals a child in Mark 5:41. CSM's proficiency in water skiing is mentioned in passing, which is a reference to actor William B. Davis who is, in real life, a champion veteran water skier. Mulder visits his mother and Scully finds the pictures of Smith on her computer at (curiously enough) 11:21. Happy birthday, Mrs Carter!

Executive Producers: Chris Carter, R. J. Goodwin, Howard Gordon
Producers: Joseph Patrick Finn, Kim Manners, Rob Bowman
Associate Producer: Lori Jo Nemhauser
Consulting Producers: Ken Horton, James Wong, Glen Morgan
Co-Producers: Paul Rabwin, Vince Gilligan, Frank Spotnitz
Additional Cast: Laurie Holden (Marita Covarrubias)

74: Herrenvolk
First Transmission 4th October 1996
Written by Chris Carter Directed by
R. W. Goodwin

Cast:
Roy Thinnes, Morris Panych, Garvin Cross, Ken Camroux, Michael David Simms.

Story:
Fox stabs the Pilot with the Alien weapon and escapes with Smith to Canada, to find a man stung to death by bees. The Pilot was not properly killed however, and forces Scully to get him back on Smith's trail. The conspiracy tests X's loyalty by telling him that Mrs Mulder is still in danger. Skinner meanwhile is helping Mulder and has found five 'Smiths' around the country, all of whom are doing some sort of research. This work is an inventory of protein tags put into Humans as part of the Smallpox Eradication Programme, a story which the authorities find hard to believe when Scully tries to warn them. Mulder and Smith find a farm growing an unknown plant, staffed by clones of Samantha at the age she was when first taken. Hot on their trail, the badly wounded Pilot chases Smith while Mulder is left on his own and returns to his mother's side. On the advice of X, Scully has placed a guard on Mrs Mulder but this exposes X as the security leak and he is killed, writing SRSG in blood. This is revealed to stand for 'Special Representative to the Secretary General', whose assistant, Marita Covarrubias, meets Mulder in New York, giving him photographs of Samantha. CSM makes the Pilot heal Mrs Mulder, claiming that Fox must always have something to lose.

Comments:
Scully's theory about the Smallpox jabs is correct; for some reason the shapeshifters want to inventory the entire population of America. This is part of 'the process', a plan which is leading up to the colonisation of Earth by the shapeshifter race, who need the honey the bees produce as food. The clones working on the farm are like worker ants; a lot of dumb drones. Why they are all like Samantha may or may not be relevant, because there is no good reason why they would want to draw attention to themselves with a farm full of clones unless they had to. The involvement of the Special Representative means that they have UN backing though, so this shouldn't be a problem. Smith too is a clone, but a higher-level one who can speak and seemingly has all the powers of an individual shapeshifter - except he is immune to the bee sting, while the Pilot is not, so the assassin may be a 'genuine' shapeshifter. Mulder, for some reason, is a vital part of the plan but what this could be is anybody's guess.

75: Home
First Transmission 11th October 1996
Written by Morgan & Wong Directed by
Kim Manners

Cast:

Tucker Smallwood, Chris Nelson Norris, Adrian Hughes, John Trotter, Karin Konoval, Sebastian Spence, Judith Maxie, Kenny James.

Story:
A deformed infant body is dug up in the rural village of Home, Pennsylvania. Suspicion falls inevitably on the three retarded brothers who live close to the burial site, but the local sheriff does not share Mulder and Scully's instincts. A high level of inbreeding is found in the baby's genetic make-up and evidence of a recent birth is found on the brother's estate, Peacock farm. After the three murder the sheriff, Mulder and Scully return with the deputy to bring them in. The deputy is killed along with two of the brothers, the third escaping with his invalid mother.

Comments:
Small-town inbreeding, murder, a monster on the loose at the end - all the ingredients for a fine episode. So how come it's an enormous pile of pants? If you missed this one first time round, congratulate yourself. There isn't any amusing trivia and just one decent scene where Mulder tenderly comforts Scully.

76: Teliko
First Transmission 18th October 1996
Written by Howard Gordon Directed by
James Charleston

Cast:
Carl Lumbly, Willie Amakye, Zakes Mokae, Maxine Guess, Bill Mackenzie, Bob Morrisey, Michael O'Shea, Danny Wattley.

Story:
Scully examines the body of an African-American who has lost all skin colour. With information from Marita the agents finds a toxic plant from West Africa and a man called Samuel Aboah, who has no pituitary gland. A minister for Burkino Faso cites the legend of Teliko; evil spirits who drain their victims of life and colour. Mulder postulates that the Teliko might be legends built up around a tribe of Africans who hunted Humans to steal their hormone glands, which would result in a dramatic loss of colour. Aboah escapes from hospital and uses a thorn to paralyse Mulder, but is shot by Scully and dies.

Comments:
Yet more points for the side of rationality and realism as ghostly entities are dispelled in favour of psychopathic mutants. Poor old Agent Pendrell is still stuck on Scully and nearly cries when he hears she has a date. In the titles, the normal slogan 'The Truth Is Out There' is replaced by 'Deceive Inveigle Obfuscate'.

77: Unruhe
First Transmission 27th October 1996
Written by Vince Gilligan Directed by
Rob Bowman

Cast:
Pruitt Taylor Vince, Sharon Alexander, Walter Marsh, Angela Donahue, William MacDonald, Ron Chartier, Michel Cram, Christopher Royal, Michelle Melland, Scott Heindl.

Story:
A particularly nasty killer is on the loose in Traverse City, Michigan; a young man is stabbed in the head and his girlfriend is kidnapped after having her photograph taken in a passport booth. When developed, it shows her screaming, surrounded by ghosts. She is soon found, but the kidnapper has performed an amateur lobotomy on her. Another woman is kidnapped by the same man and no clues are proving useful until Mulder takes photographs from the scene to be enhanced, which lead him to Gerry Schnauz, a former mental patient. Schnauz has never recovered from his sister's suicide and his attack on his father, which he blames on the 'Howlers' – spirits inside people's minds. His clumsy attempts at lobotomies are his way of trying to rid the women of these spirits. He captures Scully and is only just stopped from hacking out her frontal lobes by a timely intervention from Mulder.

Comments:
The writer may not be Carter, but this could still just have easily have been a Millenium episode. Creepy serial killers using horrifying methods to make their victims suffer are really up to Lance Henricksen these days, so why can't they just order the Millenium team in and get on with the necessary conspiracy-clobbering themselves? This is not an X-File, it's a disturbed man trying to atone for past sins. The photograph-altering is a little weird though. 'Unruhe' means 'unrest' in German (which Scully took in college).

78: The Field Where I Died
First Transmission 3rd November 1996
Written by Morgan & Wong   Directed by Rob Bowman

Cast:
Kristen Cloke, Michael Massee, Anthony Harrison, Doug Abrahams, Donna White, Michael Dobson.

Story:
The Temple of the Seven Stars are a religious cult, led by Vernon and his seven wives. The FBI raid their enclosure in Apison, Tennessee, suspecting a cache of weapons and a possibility of mass suicide. One of the wives, Melissa, is questioned by Fox and Dana. She claims to regress to some past lives which include herself, Mulder and Scully. Scully investigates the validity of her memories while Fox undergoes regression therapy and backs up her claims. The FBI continue their search for the stockpile but the cult, acting on orders from Vernon, commit suicide.

Comments:
This past lives nonsense sours the whole episode, which could have been a really good look at the influence these cult leaders have over otherwise rational adults. Once again Scully seems to have got it right – Melissa is suffering from multiple personality disorder (and drags the alarmingly gullible Mulder in with her).

79: Sanguinarium
First Transmission 10th November 1996
Written by Valerie & Vivian Mayhew
Directed by Kim Manners

Cast:
Richard Beymer, O-Lan Jones, Arlene Mazerolle, Gregory Thirloway, John Juliani, Paul Raskin, Andrew Airlie, Marie Stillin, Norman Armour, Martin Evans.

Story:
A patient dies while the doctor claims he is having an out-of-body experience in Greenwood Memorial Hospital and Mulder believes the physician was possessed, having seen evidence of a pentagram in the operating theatre. A nurse then uncharacteristically attacks another doctor before dying, having ingested hundreds of needles. More deaths follow which echo a pattern last seen ten years ago, which leads the investigation to Dr Franklin. He is killing patients born on the Witches Sabbat in order to gain a new identity every ten years, and completes his new transformation despite Mulder and Scully's attempts to stop him, escaping with a new face.

Comments:
Franklin uses black magic to perform all sorts of disgusting deeds, most usefully the ability to transport objects into people's bodies and to control their will. The new face he gains every so often must be some way for him to achieve immortality via the black arts, which in itself is a wonderful critique of the plastic surgery industry. The whole show points a very damning finger at the idea of cosmetic enhancement (Mulder spends a lot of time wondering whether he should get a nose job. Well ladies, should he?) and as Scully says, "There is magic going on here...only it's being done with silicon, collagen and a well-placed scalpel." Sounds like real magic to me.....

80: Musings of a Cigarette Smoking Man
First Transmission 17th November 1996
Written by Glen Morgan   Directed by James Wong

Cast:
Morgan Weisser, Chris Owens, Donnelly Rhodes, Dan Zukhovic, Peter Hanlon, Dean Aylesworth, Paul Jarrett, David Fredericks, Laurie Murdoch.

Story:
CSM enjoys a few nostalgic memories as he spies on the offices of the Lone Gunmen talking with Mulder and Scully. Frohike says he knows who CSM is and what he wants to be. CSM remembers various events in his life in the conspiracy – he assassinated JFK and Martin Luther King, has been present at Alien executions and is responsible for just about every significant event in the world since the war, not to mention the force behind the Oscars and most large sporting events.

Comments:
CSM appeared on 20th August, 1940 (which would make him 13 when he appeared in the flashback with Deep Throat and Bill Mulder in 1953 during 'Apocrypha' – but then Frohike is almost certainly being vague when he claims this as a birthday). The son a Communist spy who was executed for working with the Americans, his mother died of lung cancer (as a young man he never touched cigarettes) and he grew up a lonely orphan, spending most of his time reading. Re-appearing in 1962 as an army captain with Bill Mulder, they must have met up with Deep Throat at some point and formed a covert investigative team which then became involved with the conspiracy. By 1968 CSM is superior to J. Edgar Hoover and by 1991 he is overseeing the Rodney King trial, Bosnian independence, the Oscar nominations and can call Saddam Hussain back at his leisure. He didn't actually start smoking until 1963 and his lighter is inscribed with (almost) the same Legend Fox uses as a password for his computer – 'Trust No One'. We learn some interesting trivia this episode – Mulder's first words were 'JFK' and CSM is actually a scorned author whose trashy crime novels were summarily rejected by publishers. Lee Oswald called him 'Mr Hunt', but this must be a failed attempt at a joke by the writers as it's a reference to Howard Hunt, a real CIA agent involved

with Watergate and allegedly the JFK assassination.
Deep Throat quotes Security Council Resolution 10-
13. Happy birthday, Chris!

81: Tunguska
First Transmission 24th November 1996
Written by Spotnitz & Carter
Directed by Kim Manners

Cast:
Fritz Weaver, Malcolm Stewart, David
Bloom, Campbell Lane, Stefan
Arngrim, Brent Stait.

Story:
Acting on a tip-off, the FBI
set a trap for a terrorist
group and capture Alex
Krycek. He claims he is the
one who sent the informa-
tion to Mulder and wants
revenge on CSM. He gives
Fox and Scully more leads
which they follow to a
courier bag containing a
meteor fragment. Mulder
restrains Krycek in
Skinner's apartment and
meets Marita, who arranges
for him to go to the bag's
ultimate destination —
Russia. He takes Alex with
him as he speaks Russian.
The fragment is inhabited by
the Alien slime from
'Apocrypha' and Scully stays
in the USA to investigate several deaths of people unfortunate enough to have come into
close contact with it. Before she
can find anything useful, she and
Skinner are called up for a Congress
investigation into the death of the
courier, whom Krycek killed in
Skinner's home. In the northern wastes
of Siberia, Mulder and Alex find a slave
labour camp and are captured. Mulder wakes
up to find himself being sprayed by what
looks like Alien slime.

Comments:
The title is named after the mysterious explosion
in 1908, long been rumoured to have been a UFO crash-
landing or some such event. This episode takes up
the baton and claims that the rock, previously
thought to be an ancient meteorite, is from the
Siberian explosion which must have been the vehicle
used then by the Alien oil. Good to see Skinner vent-
ing some of his pent-up frustration on the helpless
Krycek, who was freed from his coffin by the terrorists he now works for.

82: Terma
First Transmission 1st December 1996
Written by Spotnitz & Carter   Directed
by Rob Bowman

Cast:
Stefan Arngrim, Jan Rubes, Fritz Weaver, Brent
Strait, Malcolm Stewart, Campbell Lane, Robin
Mossley, Brenda McDonald, Pamela MacDonald, Eileen
Pedde, Jessica Shcreier.

Story:
A Russian agent goes to the USA and murders the Well-
Manicured Man's doctor, a woman who WMM is also hav-
ing an affair with. Mulder and Krycek make it out of
the camp (Alex loses an arm in the process) while
Scully is briefly put in jail for contempt of
Congress. The Russian agent kills a scientist infect-

ed with 'Black Cancer' from the slime and steals the
meteor fragment. Mulder and Scully reunite in the USA
and try to retrieve the rock, but it is sent deep
underground by an explosion.

Comments:
The slime
living in the
rock and used by
the Russians in their
experiments seems to be
subtly different from the
one seen in 'Apocrypha' — it is
just as deadly, but does not appear
to be intelligent in any way. Whatever
it is, everyone wants to have it and to use
it as a biological weapon, from the USA and the
Russians to Saddam Hussain (which is why the troops
in the Gulf were given anti-biowarfare shots). The
experiments done by the conspiracy in Florida are to
make a cure for the 'Black Cancer' which the slime
causes (and which Mulder is unaffected by — the evidence for him being non-human mounts). In the title
squence, the slogan 'The Truth Is Out There' is
replaced with 'E Pur si Muove'.

83: Paper Hearts
First Transmission 15th December 1996
Written by Vince Gilligan Directed by
Rob Bowman

Cast:
Tom Noonan, Byrne Piven, Vanessa Morely, Sonia
Norris, Carly McKillip, Paul Bittante, John Dadey.

Story:
Mulder is plagued by strange dreams that lead
him to the unmarked grave of a murdered
young girl; an old killing perpetrated by John Lee Roche, a serial killer whom Fox has
already put in prison -
his trademark was to
strangle little
girls and take a
heart-shaped
cut of
their
cloth-
ing
as a trophy.
More dreams lead him to the trophy stash, where he
finds sixteen hearts - three more than Roche confessed to and thus meaning two more bodies lie undiscovered. Scully and Mulder interview the killer in
prison, where Roche reveals he knows about Mulder's
sister. Mulder has a dream in which the night of
Samantha's abduction is replayed, but instead of an
Alien, Roche comes to take her. He returns to him in
jail and loses control when Roche refuses to co-oper-
ate, punching him in the face. Not knowing what to
believe anymore, Mulder goes to his family home and
finds the exact model of vacuum cleaner that Roche
sold to Bill Mulder all those years ago, proving he
was in the area at the right time. Fox is let back
in to see Roche, who demands his trophies back in
return for further help. These Mulder provides, but
Roche is playing with Mulder and after inviting him
to select Samantha's 'remains', says he will only
help if taken to the scene of the crime. Mulder does
so without the proper authorisation and Roche
describes the house in detail once they are there,
claiming to recognise it all - but Mulder has tricked
him, it is a different house and Roche is exposed as
a liar. During the pair's stay in a motel, Roche
escapes and Mulder awakes to find himself cuffed, his
gun and badge missing and Skinner with Scully thump-
ing his door. Roche has taken off but cannot resist
one more girl whom he saw earlier. Mulder uses his
profiling skills to predict where Roche will take his
prey and finds them. Roche is shot dead, taking his
secrets with him.

Comments:
It's 'Pusher' and 'Aubrey' revisited with the crime
fighter led to the ancient scene of the crime by
dreams and influenced by a weirdo with abnormal
mental powers. The attempt to re-write Mulder's
personal history is striking when compared to
the end-of-season finale but doesn't really
leave anyone convinced at this stage.
Mulder's theory that his profile of Roche
all those years ago (one of the first
criminals Mulder worked on) opened
some kind of two-way information
transit is lamentably poor.

84: El Mundo Gira
First Transmission 12th
January 1997
Written by John Shiban
Directed by Tucker
Gates

Cast:
Ruben Blades, Raymond Cruz,
Pamela Diaz, Jose Yenque,
Lillian Hurst, Susan Bain,
Robert Thurston, Simi, Tina
Amayo, Mike Kopsa.

Story:
A pair of lovelorn Hispanic
brothers, Eladio and
Soledad, are thrown into dis-
array when the object of
their affections, Maria, is
killed during a freak rain of
yellow water and her goats are
mutilated. Eladio goes missing
soon afterwards. Flakita, the
neighbourhood gossip, claims
Eladio has become El Chupacabra - the
legendary 'goatsucker' responsible
for numerous livestock mutilations and
said to resemble a Grey Alien. Conrad
Lozano, an immigration officer, helps Mulder
find and incarcerate Eladio, who protests his
innocence while Scully does the autopsy on Maria's
body - she was killed by a deadly fungal infection
which spread and grew at phenomenal speeds. Eladio
escapes custody and another victim of the fungus is
found before they catch up with him at a construc-
tion site. His brother Soledad is also there, seeking revenge for Maria's death and both evade cap-

ture, fleeing to the shanty town. Another death by fungus gives the scientists the answers they need and Scully warns Mulder of the dangers involved - an unknown but very powerful enzyme is responsible for the extraordinary fungal growth and Eladio appears to be a carrier. Eladio gets some help from his cousin Gabrielle and sees his face in the mirror - he has been transformed into El Chupacabra and does indeed resemble a Grey. His brother Soledad is still after vengeance and the two go to meet for a showdown, the FBI agents hot on their trail. What happened that night can only be guessed at - Flakita tells of how Lozano arranged a meeting between the brothers but 'El Chupacabras' descended from the sky, killing Lozano and taking Soledad away. Gabrielle claims that Lozano was shot accidentally during the fight between the brothers, who overcame their differences and fled to Mexico, both now looking like El Chupacabra. Skinner is left to puzzle over Mulder and Scully's inconclusive report.

Comments:
A refreshing take on the monster-meets-Alien story, as the legend of El Chupacabra is quite real to many people in South America and examples of similar monsters can be found in the folklore of many nations. It is a bit fanciful to link it to the Aliens however, as accounts of the beast's appearance are conflicting - a four-legged animal with strange appendages on it's head is more common than the upright Grey. If this is evidence of an Alien incursion in the X-Files universe, then it seems to show the Greys in a new light - are they deliberately killing goats and people with this strange enzyme, or is it some way of getting Humans to become Greys? Is it the work of the conspiracy, who have made a breakthrough and can now turn people into mutants just by dropping this yellow rain on them?

85: Leonard Betts
First Transmission 26th January 1997
Written by Spotnitz, Shiban & Gilligan
Directed by Kim Manners

Cast:
Jennifer Clement, Paul McCrane, Lucia Walters, Marjorie Lovett, Ken Jones, Sean Campbell, Greg Newmeyer, Dave Hurtubise, Bill Dow, Brad Loree, Peter Bryant, Don Ackerman, Laara Sadiq, J. Douglas Stewart.

Story:
Betts, an ambulance worker, is decapitated in an accident. His headless body is reanimated and walks out of the hospital. His head miraculously grows back, because he is a mutant with a difference - in a new leap for evolution, he has become a living cancer, the tumour having integrated itself into his cellular structure. The downside is that to live, he must feed off other people's 'normal' tumours. Scully and Mulder find his head in the hospital's disposal unit and analyse it, finding out the truth about his cancerous state. His previous partner, Michele Wilkes, finds the newly-regrown Betts working for another company but he kills her to avoid discovery. The crime is witnessed and he is left handcuffed while Fox and Dana arrive, but before they can get there he rips off his own thumb to escape. In his car are found packages of human tumours, his source of sustenance. Betts, weak with hunger, attacks and feeds off a smoking man and reproduces, making a copy of himself. At Betts' mother's house (Mrs Tanner), they find a lead that takes them to a storage facility where they find the body of Leonard's last victim and also Betts himself, who tries to run them down in his car. He fails, and the car explodes, taking 'Betts' with it. Suspecting the truth, Mulder stakes out Mrs Tanner's house, where they find the old woman still alive but with a deep scalpel wound in her chest. Back at the hospital, Scully is left

alone and attacked by Betts, who was hiding on the roof of the ambulance. She kills him with the defibrillation pads.

Comments:
The prophecy of the abducted women's group in 'Nisei' comes true as Scully is revealed to be a victim of the experimentation suffered at the hands of the conspiracy. Let's hope there are some new basic plot-

lines discovered in the Fox TV vault before too long, or every X-Files episode will be unfairly compared to an earlier one. This is just 'Tooms' all over again with very little in the way of added gloss. But disgustingly lovely nonetheless.....

86: Never Again
First Transmission 2nd February 1997
Written by Morgan and Wong   Directed by Rob Bowman

Cast:
Rodney Rowland, Carla Stewart, Barry "Bear" Hortin, Igor Morozov, Jan Bailey Mattia, Rita Bozi, Marilyn Chin, Jillian Fargey, B. J. Harrison, Natasha Vasiluk, Bill Croft, Peter Nadler, Jen Forgie, Jay Donohue, Ian Robison.

Story:
Our heroes take a sabbatical from FBI work and the X-Files in this episode, as Mulder goes on a spiritual journey to Graceland, Memphis and Scully is left on her own. Mulder insists she looks into a Russian man thought to have some information on UFO's and they argue before parting on bad terms. Scully, having nothing better to do, grudgingly goes to inves-

tigate the man whom she quickly learns is a fraud and an extortionist. During her follow-up she meets Ed Jerse, a recent divorcee who had a tattoo of a woman and the words 'Never again' on his arm which has since begun taunting him and calling him a loser. Before he realised it was the tattoo, he had been driven to extreme violence and had killed a woman (Scully met him when he was in the parlour to try and get the design covered over). He and Scully hit

it off and she goes out with him, getting drunk and having her own tattoo done. Back at Ed's apartment, she notices his tattoo is bleeding - it tells Ed not to touch her or she's dead. The next morning, Ed is gone and detectives arrive, telling Scully about the homicide of the woman Jerse killed and of the blood abnormalities they found - it is just a routine follow-up however and Ed is not a suspect yet. When he returns, Scully tells him of the news and he goes crazy, knocking her out and taking her to the incinerator. She wakes up and urges him to take control, whereupon he holds his arm in the incinerator and burns off the tattoo. The blood seeping from his tattoo earlier had been found to contain a hallucinogen, used by the Russian tattooist.

Comments:
Just as Mulder went overboard in 'Grotesque', so here Scully does the same thing. The relationship between Mulder and Scully is a lot more uncertain this series as they settle back into the close working relationship that was so apparent in the first and second season, but with Scully showing a more assertive side. Scully's self-analysis is very accurate - she is doomed to repeat the sequence of following a father figure until it becomes too much and rebellion is the only means of escape. The voice of the

tattoo is provided by Jodie Foster and the body art selected by Scully is an Uroboros, the symbol of eternity used in the title sequence of 'Millenium'.

87: Memento Mori
First Transmission 9th February 1997
Written by Carter, Spotnitz, Shiban & Gilligan
Directed by Rob Bowman

Cast:
Gillian Barber, David Lovgren, Julie Bond, Morris Panych, Sean Allen.

Story:
Scully tells Mulder of her cancer and they go to see the women from 'Nisei' who suffered from the same disease. Only one of them remains alive, Penny Northern, who is hospitalised by her condition. Back at the house of another recently-deceased victim of the same cancer, Betsy Hagopian, they find that her computer files are being downloaded. Tracing the call, they find Kurt Crawford who says he was doing it to prevent the files from being destroyed by the conspiracy. Scully visits Penny in hospital and turns to a Dr Scanlon, who says he has isolated the condition and may be able to treat it. Fox and Dana find that all the women attended the same fertility clinic in Pennsylvania, which Mulder goes to investigate. There he finds Kurt again - unaware that back in Allentown, the Kurt he left to look after Scully has been killed by the Grey-Haired Man (the assassin of X) and dissolved into a pool of green slime. At the clinic, Fox and the other Kurt download a file connected to Scully, but cannot find any more useful information. Mulder tries to contact CSM through Skinner but Walter refuses (but secretly tries to ask the enigmatic conspiracy member without Fox knowing). Fox then enlists the help of the Gunmen, who go with him to infiltrate the clinic's mainframe which is housed in a top-secret facility. Once inside, Mulder finds out that Dr Scanlon is a member and sends word to Scully to stop her treatment, and finds the other Kurt clones to his surprise. They are doctors there, working on an incubator containing Human forms, one of whom Mulder recognises as Samantha. A Kurt clone shows Fox a storage room full of Human ova taken from the abducted women, including Scully. The Kurts are working on a way to save their birth-mothers. Mulder is almost killed by the Grey-Haired Man but escapes thanks to the Gunmen, only to find Penny has since died and Scully is determined to continue life as normal.

Comments:
The truth of the experiments is finally revealed - Scully and her fellow abductees are the birth-mothers of Alien/Human hybrid clones, a foetus of which was seen in 'The Erlenmyer Flask'. The process requires intense radiation, which results in all the women developing cancer (this may be the main reason for developing a radiation-resistant Human strain). These are the Samanthas and identical Doctors as seen in 'Colony' and possibly the origins of the Jeremiah Smith's as well. Since this is clearly the conspiracy at work, we can only assume that the shapeshifters accept some level of experimentation with their DNA, as long as they can exercise complete control over it. Scully makes some sweeping statements about cancer being modern science's equivalent of possession and chemotherapy our version of exorcism, which is all a pile of over-philosophised nonsense really.

88: Kaddish
First Transmission 16th February 1997
Written by Howard Gordon   Directed by Kim Manners

Cast:

Justine Micelli, David Groh, Harrison Coe, Channon Roe, Jabin Litweniec, Timur Karabilgin, Jonathan Whittaker, David Wohl, George Gordon, Murrey Rabinovitch, Daviv Freedman.

Story:
Shopkeeper Isaac Luria is murdered in a Hasidic Jewish community, days before he was to marry Ariel Luria in a Jewish ceremony (she bears his name because they obtained a marriage license beforehand). Mulder and Scully investigate the death, which is the result of a race-hate beating committed by three youths. One of these boys is then found strangled, but the fingerprints at the scene are those of Isaac Luria. The maker of a race-hate pamphlet is questioned about the deaths and listening in are the remaing boys, Banks and Macguire. Unnerved by the prospect of Isaac returning from the dead, they dig up his grave but only find what should be there - Isaac's dead body. Macguire is killed, his body found under a pile of mud. Stumped, Fox turns to Kenneth Ungar, a scholar of Jewish mysticism who tells him of the legend of the "Golem" and how a likeness of a man made in earth may be constructed and animated. Mulder and Scully find Weiss, Ariel's father, in the attic of a synagogue where Banks is hanging lifeless from the rafters. He admits to the murders of the boys and is put in prison. This does not stop the printer of the anti-semitic leaflets, Carl Brunjes, being killed and Weiss is released, only to find his daughter preparing for an orthodox marriage ceremony. He tries to stop her but the Golem brushes him aside. Mulder tries to intervene but he too is swept away by the clay man, who places the ring on Ariel's finger. She wipes away some writing on the golem's hand and it disintegrates.

Comments:
A modern look at the age old Jewish legend of the Golem, the clay slave whose origins started in the old Jewish quarter of Prague. Said to have been created by the city's top Rabbi as a helper for menial duties, it ran amok and was never seen again - although tourist guides will tell you that in the ancient Synagogue, strange sounds can be heard from the attic from time to time, so it's nice to see that the writers are sticking to a real myth. The authentic Golem is powered by a piece of paper inside it's head, on which is written it's instructions in Hebrew - it is not and never has been a vehicle for spirits, but rather an early version of Frankensteins' monster. Scully, of course, is unavoidably detained just long enough to miss seeing the Golem while Mulder gets knocked about by it with wonderful abandon.

89: Unrequited
First Transmission 23rd February 1997
Written by Gordon & Carter Directed by
Michael Lange

Cast:
Scott Hylands, Peter Lacroix, Ryan Michael, Don McWilliams, Bill Agnew, Mark Holden, Larry Musser, Lesley Ewen, Allan Franz, William Nunn, William Taylor, Jen Jasey.

Story:
Lieutanant General Peter MacDougal is killed by a shot at close range while being driven in his limo. The only possible suspect is the chauffeur, a member of a right-wing paramilitary group "Right Hand". Tests show he did not do it however, so the agents take a closer look at the group's activities. It is led by an ex-marine called Denny Markham, who tells the FBI of a Green Beret called Teager, who has spent twenty five years as a POW and was only just liberated in 1995 - he subsequently disappeared, but is later seen by Renee Davenport, a woman at the Vietnam Veteran's Memorial. He disappears from her in plain

view, but she is diagnosed as having a floating blind spot. Mulder's investigations lead him to General Steffan, who along with MacDougal signed Teager's death certificate. Steffan is killed by Teager despite being protected by several agents. Marita steps in to lend a hand and tells Mulder that MacDougal, Steffan and a third man were part of a group responsible for the liquidation of South Vietnamese sodliers who helped the US and that their testimony would have been vital to the calculation of reparations - meaning that the government is quite happy to see them being taken out. Covarrubias gives him the name of the third General, Bloch, who is about to address the crowd for the memorial's re-dedication. Mulder heads a group of agents and Teager is spotted in the audience, but he vanishes in broad daylight while Bloch is rushed to his limo. Skinner just saves his life by knocking him to the floor as Teager fires from inside the limo and he is shot as he tries to make his escape.

Comments:
Okay, so how did he do it? There are some off-hand remarks about the ability of the Viet-Cong to vanish at will, but it's just a war-myth to explain why they were so darn tricky to find and shoot. Apart from Teager's rather nifty ability to copy what ancient radio-play hero The Shadow could do, there's no reason for this to be an X-File or for it to be in this series. But if it gets Skinner out of his office, we can only be grateful.

90: Tempus Fugit
First Transmission 16th March 1997
Written by Carter & Spotnitz Directed by Rob Bowman

Cast:
Joe Spano, Tom O'Brien, Scott Bellis, Chilton Crane, Brendan Beiser, Greg Michaels, Robert Moloney, Felicia Schulman, Rick Dobran, Jerry Schram, David Palffy, Mark Wilson, Marek Wieldman, Jon Raitt.

Story:
A surprise birthday party for Scully at the Headless Woman's Pub is interrupted by the arrival of Sharon Graffia, who says she is the sister of Max Fenig (from season 1 episode 'Fallen Angel'). He has just died in an airplane crash and told his sister to contact Mulder or Scully if something should happen to him. The agents attend the crash meeting, headed by Mike Millar, who plays the tape of the pilot's last words - Mulder notes the mention of an intercept craft, but his theory that the flight was forced down is derided by the experts. At the crash site Fox notices a nine-minute discrepancy on the passengers' watches and the time that the crash was supposed to have occurred. Another investigator, Garett, uses an acid spray to remove all identifying features from a body, while the others concentrate on rescuing a survivor from the wreckage - Scully finds he has been exposed to intense radiation. Max Fenig's body is found. Fox and Dana interview the Air Force traffic controllers who were on duty at the time of the incident, Louis Frish and Armando Gonzales, neither of whom had any contact with the airliner. Louis later finds Gonzales' body and narrowly escapes death via a government hit-squad himself, by hiding on the control-tower roof. He finds the agents with Millar and reveals that he had been forced to lie by his superiors - there was an unknown blip on the radar that had approached flight 549, but it exploded and brought down the commercial craft with it. Fox believes that a third aircraft must have shot the interceptor down. All four of them are then drawn into a car chase, which they escape from. Millar sees a UFO above the crash site and Sharon, previously missing, is discovered there dazed and confused. Scully and Louis retire to the Headless Woman's Pub and have a shoot-out with Garrett - Agent Pendrell

is shot in the chest in the crossfire. Mulder is out scuba-diving, on the grounds that the interceptor must have landed in the Great Sacandaga Lake as no other crash site can be found. He finds wreckage and the body of a Grey, but before he can do anything else he is blinded by a bright light...

Comments:
See next episode (if you know what's good for you).

91: Max
First Transmission 23rd March 1997
Written by Carter & Spotnitz   Directed by Kim Manners

Cast:
As last episode

Story:
The lights approaching Mulder underwater are from military frogmen and their submersibles, who place him under arrest. Garrett escapes the shoot-out but Louis is taken into custody for interfering with a federal investigation. Pendrell dies from his wounds. An official story is released, stating that the airliner collided with an Air Force jet which was wrongfully directed by Louis. Sharon is exposed as a pathological liar who met Fenig in a mental institution. Max's mobile home is searched and clues lead to an object which Max claimed was incontrovertible proof that the Air Force was using Alien technology. There was originally one such artifact which was taken from Max and Sharon. She stole the original from her employers, which was split into three parts – only the third remains undiscovered, but Mulder follows Max's clues and finds it. Intending to take it back to Washington with him, Garrett follows him on board to try and steal it – Fox overpowers him but during the flight, a UFO appears and Garrett seizes the evidence in the confusion despite Mulder's pleas for him to drop it as the UFO draws near. Garrett never makes it to Washington and Mulder comes back empty-handed.

Comments:
The conspiracy takes a back seat as the good old Air Force comes into it's own, employing the same dirty intimadatory tactics. Proof positive that Alien technology is being put to practical, Human-serving needs rather than the darker purpose of colonisation. The technology used is that of the Greys, which has so far proven superior to that of the shapeshifters (if indeed it is two different races we are dealing with), of whom the USAF does not appear to have any knowledge of. Mulder's explanation of events – that the UFO was shot down by the Air Force and took the airplane with it – must be true given what happened to Garrett. He was probably working for the conspiracy, covering up the evidence of a previous conspiracy agent who tried to recover the evidence Max was carrying and prevent the USAF from using it. If he was working for the USAF, they would have known a UFO would try to take the artifact and taken pre-emptive measures to ensure an uninterrupted flight – if it was so easy to shoot down last time, another would be no problem. If not, there are some major plot holes at large (oh dear!). The Greys seem to be just trying to protect their own interests here – understandable when a civilisation that wants to shoot you down on sight gets hold of your technology. There is also some more lost time here but everyone is conscious through it, so we can discount rumours that Mulder and Scully have been abducted each time there is some temporal discrepancy. Poor old Pendrell looks longingly at Scully for the last time, which is an unjust way of saying to all male fans that Scully is way out of your league. Oh, to be her holster just for one scene etc etc.

92: Synchrony
First Transmission 13th April 1997
Written by Howard Gordon & David Greenwalt
Directed by Jim Charleston

Cast:
Jed Rees, Jospeh Fuqua, Michael Fairman, Hiro Kanagwa, Jonathan Walker, Brent Chapman, Eric Buermeyer, Patricia Idlette, Austin Basile, Alison Matthews.

Story:
An elderly man tries to warn Lucas Menand, a research student, that he will be knocked down and killed that night at 11:46 precisely. He and his friend Jason Nichols call campus security and the old man is driven away, but minutes later Menand is run down by a bus at the time the man predicted. Scully and Mulder question Nichols, who was seen pushing Menand into the road but he claimed he was trying to save Lucas after the old man's warning. The guard who drove the man away is found frozen to death, caused by a freezing agent injected into him according to Scully. Nichols says that he was arguing with Menand over claims that he had falsified research data. The elderly man pops up again and kills a Japanese researcher, Dr Yonechi by injecting him with the freezing compound. Fox and Dana talk to Jason's girlfriend Lisa, who recognises the compound as one which Nichols has been trying to synthesise for years – but it hasn't been invented yet. They try to resuscitate Yonechi but he bursts into flames. Lisa confesses she has been falsifying the data and Jason took the blame for it – the only people who could expose her were Menand and Yonechi, now dead. The agents catch up with the old man and find a crumpled old photograph in his room which shows Yonechi, Lisa and Jason celebrating their success – five years in the future. The old man is Jason Nichols, coming back to the past to alter the future. Lisa finds the old man and he injects her, but she is saved by Scully who manages to correctly revive her this time. The young Nichols finds his older self trying to erase vital computer files and the two struggle – the older man bursts into flames, killing both him and his younger self. Lisa sets to work on completing the compound.

Comments:
The freezing formula is a prerequisite for time travel, though exactly why is never made clear despite some interesting real science being explained. The special effects are rather nicely done as well. A clever episode, were it not for the fact that the premise is as old as the hills amongst the Sci-fi set. For a much more original take on this idea, try seeking out Ray Bradbury's short story 'A Touch Of Petulance' written years before the X-Files came about.

93: Small Potatoes
First Transmission 20th April 1997
Written by Vince Gilligan   Directed by Clifford Bole

Cast:
Christine Cavanaugh, Constance Barnes, Carrie Cain Sparks, Monica Gemmer, Darin Morgan, P. Lynn Johnson, David Cameron.

Story:
In the small town of Martinsburg, West Virginia, a baby born with a tail becomes part of a statistical impossibility when four other babies are born with the same defect. All five women used the same fertility clinic so the agents make their way through the angry new parents to find a very confused Dr Alton Pugh, who claims he never even gave them anything yet. Mulder finds and chases a man with a scar on his behind consistent with the removal of a ves-

tigial tail during infancy and tests show he is the father of all five children - yet all the women protest that they have never slept with anyone but their husbands. When the man, Eddie Van Blundht, escapes from the county jail by changing his appearance to look like the deputy, it becomes clear that he used this talent to look like the husbands and sire the children. Unable to find him, the duo head to Eddie's house where they talk to his father, an old circus performer who used his tail for a living as a sideshow attraction. They realise too late that they are in fact talking to Eddie Jnr and he escapes, but they find in the house the body of old Eddie Snr with full tail intact. An autopsy reveals that his entire skin formed a muscle, a feature which Eddie Jnr must have inherited and which enables him to control his appearance. He then changes himself to look like Mulder and goes to the hospital to see an old conquest, Amanda Neligan (whom he appeared to as Mark Hamill, claiming he was Luke Skywalker) but the real Mulder arrives too. Eddie locks Fox in the boiler room and returns to Washington with Scully to 'be' Mulder for a while. He turns up at Scully's doorstep with a bottle of wine and they are on the verge of getting facially attached before the real Mulder arrives and foils the scam. Eddie is thrown in prison and put on muscle relaxants to stop him from changing again.

Comments:
Season 4 may have been patchy up to now, but this one is a true gem. No Aliens, no life-threatening monsters, just Darin Morgan in front of camera giving a touching performance as a man trying in his own way to give some women what they want. Duchovny plays the part of the fake Mulder perfectly, giving his super-cool image the comedown it so desparately needs ("Are you lookin' at me?"). Mulder's essential solitude is brought into sharp focus as his life is laid bare by Eddie - an answerphone message from a sex line? Please, Mulder. And Scully's right there, you idiot! And all it took was a bottle of wine and some childhood reminiscing.....

94: Zero Sum
First Transmission 27th April 1997
Written by Gordon & Spotnitz Directed by Kim Manners

Cast:
Lisa Stewart, Nicolle Nattrass, Fred Keating, Allan Gary, Theresa Puskar, Barry Creene, Paul McLean, John Moore, Laurie Holden.

Story:
A worker at a mail sorting company is killed when she encounters a swarm of bees in the toilet. Detective Ray Thomas thinks the case warrants the attention of the X-Files and E-mails details to Mulder, but Skinner intercepts them and deletes the file, before heading off to the scene. He removes all evidence of the bee attack, burns the body and replaces a blood sample in the hospital with a pre-prepared one. He meets Thomas and says he is Fox Mulder, but the case does not merit his attention. Mulder visits Skinner and tells him that someone is trying to keep him off a case involving a bee-sting death and that Detective Thomas has been shot dead. Skinner confronts CSM, who tells him that it was his fault Thomas had to die. Skinner gets into deeper trouble when he realises his gun is missing and decides to get some evidence of his own, taking a section of honeycomb from the rest room where the death occurred. Entomologist Peter Valdespino examines the larvae but is killed when they attack him - the cause of death is smallpox. Skinner uses this information to save a group of schoolchildern who are stung by the bees, but then is caught up in events as security camera footage reveals him to be the person seen talking to Thomas shortly before he was killed. Fox accuses Skinner of being in league with CSM and Walter S. goes off to find the chain-smoking conspirator for an angry confrontation. CSM meets with the elders again, where he meets Marita Covarrubias and tells her to give Mulder what he wants to hear.

Comments:
Didn't Deep Throat tell you to trust no one? Didn't he? And now look what happens. The bee sub-plot looks like being different from the shapeshifter plan to provide food, as this lot appear to orignate from the Human conspiracy's aim to make biological weapons - these insects would make an ideal agent to spread smallpox. Scully's cancer is becoming more evident as a factor in her everyday life, hard as it may seem to believe that she has a fatal disease. If the bees are a device to be used by the Aliens for colonisation, it's not a very good one as Skinner shows that smallpox can be treated with advance warning.

95: Elegy
First Transmission 4th May 1997
Written by John Shiban Directed by Jim Charleston

Cast:
Steven M. Porter, Alex Bruhanski, Sydney Lassick, Nancy Fish, Daniel Kamin, Lorena Gale, Mike Puttonen, Christine Willes, Ken Tremblett, Gerry Naim.

Story:
The image of a young girl appears to Angie Pintero in his bowling alley, moments before the same girl is found murdered outside in the street. Mulder and Scully investigate this and three other sightings of young girls before their murder is discovered and find the words 'She is me' written on the bowling lane in which Pintero saw the first one. A 911 call made from a mental hospital delivers a message from an anonymous source of the latest murder, claiming that the apparition of the girl was saying 'She is me'. The call is traced to Harold Spuller, a patient at the New Horizon Psychiatric Centre, who could be the killer but Mulder, of course, does not believe so. Scully gets a nosebleed and goes to the Ladies room where she sees a vision of a girl, silently trying to speak to her and is then told by Mulder that another victim has been found. Mulder chases Spuller to a room behind the bowling alley where he finds the obsessive man amongst thousands of scorecards - it is these which provide him with a link to the women who were killed, women whom he worshipped from afar. Harold then sees another ghost, this time of his boss at the bowling alley, Angie Pintero - rushing outside, he finds him just dead from a heart attack. Mulder takes Spuller back to the institution, where he tells Scully that everybody who saw the visions was about to die, so Harold may be next. Back inside, Harold is tormented by Nurse Innes and she is found moments later, cut and bruised with Spuller nowhere to be seen. Another patient tells Scully that Innes was poisoning Harold, so Dana confronts her in the rest room. Innes goes crazy and pulls a scalpel on her, forcing Scully to shoot her. Innes had been taking Spuller's medication, which drove her psychotic and made her kill the women to stop Harold's happiness. He is later found dead, due to the sudden withdrawal of the slow poison which Innes had been giving him.

Comments:
What's going on here? Steven M. Porter looks as if Jim Charleston gave him a copy of 'Rain Man' and told him to copy Dustin Hoffman, so stereotypical a view of a disturbed man do we have here. Somebody forgot to tell Shiban that revelations at the end of a story should bear some relation to the rest of the plot - it's like Nurse Innes was just thrown in for the last five minutes as an afterthought and by the way, she

killed all those girls too. The whole episode drags it's heels disgracefully and has no redeeming features whatsoever. If they wanted to get the point of Scully's mortality across, there must have been a better script lying around than this to work on. Still, you win some, you lose some.....

96: Demons
First Transmission 11th May 1997
Written by R. W. Goodwin   Directed by Kim Manners

Cast:
Jay Acovone, Mike Nussbaum, Chris Owens, Rebecca Toolan, Andrew Johnston, Terry Jang Barclay, Vanessa Morley, Eric Breker, Rebecca Harker, Shelly Adam, Dean Aylesworth, Alex Haythorne.

Story:
Mulder has an emotionally-charged dream in which he sees his parents reacting to some terrible event - he then wakes up in a strange motel room with blood all over him and an almost-literally smoking gun with two bullets missing in his possession! Scully traces the car outside his room to Amy and David Cassandra, whose house contains pictures of an old holiday home Fox finds inexplicably familiar. The housekeeper tells them where to find the building and on the way there, Mulder is struck by a seizure during which he remembers a young CSM in his family home. Inside the house they find the bodies of Amy and David, whose blood matches that found on Mulder. He is arrested, but traces of the drug Ketamine found in his and Amy's blood account for Mulder's story of amnesia. Another officer involved shoots himself in the head and Scully finds a small scab on his hairline, identical to the one found on Amy's body. Mulder is freed when it is found that the splatter pattern of blood on his shirt does not tally with the shots fired at David and Amy and the case is closed, assumed to be a murder-suicide. Fox has another violent flashback in which he sees his mother and CSM in each other's arms. He confronts his mother but she denies everything, so Mulder drives off to see Dr Goldstein, a psychiatrist who was treating Amy Cassandra and used unconventional drug therapy to recover lost memory. Forcing the doctor to give him the treatment at gunpoint, Mulder then disappears. Scully finds him at his parent's holiday home in Quonochontaug where he is wracked by seizures and holds his gun at Scully. He fires, just missing her and Dana convinces him that the drugs pumped into him are making all his memories unreliable. He breaks down and lowers his gun.

Comments:
Now this is more like it. The shadowy hand of the conspiracy is at work here, softening Mulder up for the big whammy next episode. Ketamine (otherwise known as 'Special K') is supposed to be a very powerful hallucinogen, known for the strength of it's effect. As anyone who has tried hallucinogens will tell you (so the author has been informed), the effects are largely unpredictable and would not actually produce tailor-made paranoic seizures....but then this is the conspiracy we're talking about here, who have extended their mind-control technology to create just the right visions that will send Fox spinning into nightmarish uncertainty. Is CSM really his father? Can Fox not even trust his own mother? For how much longer will he be able to afford his life insurance payments? Answers on a postcard please.....

97: Gethsemane
First Transmission 18th May 1997
Written by Chris Carter   Directed by R. W. Goodwin

Cast:

John Finn, Matthew Walker, James Sartorius, Pat Skipper, John Oliver, Charles Cioffi, Steve Makha, Nancy Kerr, Barry W. Levy, Arnie Wlaters, Rob Freeman, Craig Burnanski.

Story:
Scully arrives at Mulder's apartment, which is full of officers investigating a crime scene. She identifies a body there. She then appears before FBI Section Chief Scott Blevins and tells him that during her four years of working with Mulder on the X-Files (on Blevin's orders), she can only report that they are inconclusive and illegitimate; a waste of departmental resources. In a flashback we see anthropologists Arlinsky and Babcock finding the body of an Alien encased in ice on a mountaintop. Still in flashback, we see a dinner party at the Scully household, where she finds her family trying to get her faith back on track as her health deteriorates. A phone call from Mulder sends her to the Smithsonian Institute to meet Arlinsky, who takes Mulder to the Alien site claiming that ice-core samples prove the remains are over two hundred years old. They arrive only to find that someone got there before them and shot the recovery team, the Alien body missing and no clues as to what happened. They find Babcock who tells them that he buried the corpse under his tent. Back in the lab, Scully is examining the ice samples when she is attacked and thrown down the stairs by a man who turns out to be Michael Kritschgau, a Pentagon research official. He is arrested but tells Scully that if he ends up in jail, the same people who gave her cancer will kill him. Back at the mountain, Mulder and Arlinsky move the body to a warehouse where a full autopsy can be performed, but Fox is drawn away by Scully who wants him to hear Kritschgau's story - in his absence, the mountaintop assassin finds and kills Arlinsky and Babcock. Michael tells Mulder that a governmental body has been creating elaborate hoaxes to draw attention from itself - including the Alien body, which was composed of bio-materials and slowly frozen into place. Returning to the warehouse, Mulder finds the murdered anthropologists and no trace of the Alien cadaver. Mulder is overwhelmed to hear Scully tell him that the people responsible for the hoax are the same ones who gave her cancer, in an attempt to make him believe the lie. Back in the present, Dana finishes her story by telling her bosses that she has just come from Mulder's apartment, where she identified his body after he shot himself in the head.

Comments:
There are logically only two explanations to this story: one; the conspiracy has succeeded in discrediting Mulder, even to the extent that his partner does not believe him and he no longer even believes it himself and two; that Fox is putting on a grand hoax of his own, to smoke out the truth. Either way, the 'death' of Mulder is a smokescreen and as a cliffhanger, does not have the same impact as the previous season endings. It just fizzles out with the impression that nothing much has really happened - after all, Mulder has found several pieces of evidence far more convincing than the body only to have them snatched from him at the last minute, so why should this one be any different? He must know by now that nothing can be trusted, not even his own memories, so why does he lose faith so dramatically just because a Pentagon agent tells him otherwise? There is a fifth season planned and Carter has gone on record saying it could go to at least seven, even if it is not with the original characters or his involvement in the development. He seems intent on providing ever more ludicrous solutions to the end-of-season stories, in the manner of the old Flash Gordon weeklies in which the hero would miraculously escape every time to keep on fighting the good fight. Time will tell if the conspiracy plot will ever reach a satisfactory conclusion, with or without the help of Mulder and Scully.

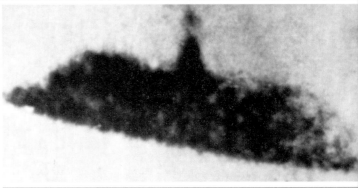

I am the God of hellfire and I give you...

The mythology of the X-Files has grown from a singular-celled organism that dwelled inside the minds of strange men into a sprawling tumour that has attacked the nervous system of public credulity. The stories that each week pretend to hold all the answers seldom fail to deliver anything but a mix of fear, curiosity and frustration in equal measure as the viewer is once more robbed of a satisfactory conclusion. In this world we are used to such inconclusive endings; it's what being a conscious animal is all about — this is why we don't like them on television. Tidy narratives with a definite ending are the rule in television programmes that have to cater to all tastes. So why is it that a mainstream show which never tells you anything has captured the attention of viewers the world over?

Another attempt to cash-in on the popularity of the alien mythology has been 'Dark Skies', which flies against the conspiratorial nature and gives you the truth straight away, right down to an eyewitness account of the Roswell landing. The hero was in fact a member of the Majestic group, the organisation that the X-Files conspiracy is loosely based on. He too had a pretty female partner, whom he got to sleep with because she was his wife. Yet this show been cancelled while the X-Files has gone from strength to strength. We don't want the truth. We can't handle the truth. Or at least, not

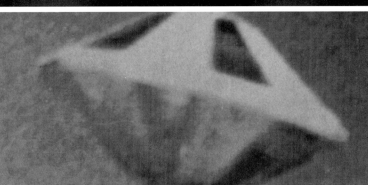

someone else's version of it....the whole point of the UFO as a focal point for twentieth century urban mythology is that it is such a vague object, shrouded in lies and half-truths so well that it would take a lifetime to sift through them all. People are able to fill this void with whatever they choose, and they have set about doing so with a feverish devotion. The Majestic-12 group shown in the Dark Skies series is an amalgamation of conspiracies based on the idea that there is an understanding between the Aliens and the government, even if it is one of open hostility. It all goes back to that fateful day back in Roswell in 1947 when, indisputably, something crashed in the deserted wastes of New Mexico. The Dark Skies version of the truth is plainly stated: a delegation of Aliens landed by prior arrangement to meet with the highest authorities, including the President, to demand their surrender. The Americans very kindly took it upon themselves to stand firm on behalf of the rest of the world and, using 1947 weaponry, shot down their craft as it beat a hasty retreat. The 'conspiracy' of this universe is a secret organisation led by Frank Bach (based on real-life man in black Dr Bloch, said to be leader of the group Majestic is based on) whose aims are to eradicate the Alien presence on Earth.

Their foe is the implacable menace of the Hive, a group consciousness of spidery creatures which can possess their Human hosts and operate in a collective. The theme is very much of the enemy within, as infected Humans are almost impossible to spot – much like the shapeshifters of the X-Files, they are a more modern take on the Bodysnatcher legend. The Greys in this universe are, like Humans, mere vehicles for the Hive to possess. The idea of the changeling as enemy is as ancient as the hills and has cropped up in fiction for years (and so-called non-fiction as well) as a good way to scare the punters when no new monster can be found. Look at other Sci-fi programmes which feature similar or same opponents: Deep Space 9 has the Dominion to worry about, led by....shapeshifters. Chief baddie in blockbuster Terminator 2? A shapeshift-

ing robot. Remember Westworld and its' sequel, Futureworld? Populated by androids, who could only be spotted by the shape of their hands. Classic Sci-fi film Bladerunner features the replicants, a bio-robot only different from it's Human creators due to it's lack of emotional response, which is shown up on a test not unlike that seen in Dark Skies before the injection goes in. It all goes back to the film that first popularised the concept, 'Invasion Of The Body Snatchers', where the pods came down and did the dirty deed.

It is nothing more than a modern-day adaptation of the age old complaint that has dogged Humanity since religion began – demonic possession. The first recorded such event in literature is in the New Testament, Mark's Gospel, where Jesus heals a man claiming to be possessed by demons. This man calls himself Legion (remember that goodness is one; evil multiform) and the devil is cast out to inhabit a flock of sheep, which later run into a river and kill themselves. That little history lesson aside, the story is essentially no different to that found in Dark Skies and can be found in many X-Files episodes, of both

the Alien and non-Alien variety. The Alien Slime of 'Apocrypha' is the most obvious example of this theme, though the ongoing implantation program is a more recent addition to the techno-myth of the saucers now that our own techniques of surgery have come into their own.

The idea of the flying disk is a recent phenomenon, not even dating from before World War II. The first such sighting was by an American pilot on a leisure flight in his light prop-driven plane during the War, on which he saw a group of unidentified aircraft flying over the Rockies. He noted their extraordinary speed (an unheard of mach 2 or 3 based on distances from peak-to-peak, which for the forties was a mind-boggling velocity) but what really struck him was their flight path; unlike an orthodox aeroplane, they skipped like saucers on the surface of a lake. Our entire mythology was built around the vagaries of linguistics (he actually reported

them to be the more aerodynamically-acceptable delta-wing shape if you really want to know) rather than any little consideration like the truth

and so the legend of the flying saucers was born. Sorry, that's all there is to it. You can look for earlier sightings, but if you find them you can bet they won't tell of anything like what we nowadays call a UFO sighting.

After this event gained national notoriety, the public's eyes were glued to the skies and sightings naturally increased dramatically. Remember when you were a kid how you'd always hear of people seeing those weird 'cigar-shaped objects' in the sky? Wonder why you don't hear about them anymore? Not because the Aliens have developed a new stealthy capability (or learned that night-flights with landing lights ablaze attracts attention), but because the cigar-shaped objects are just the fuselages of commercial airliners and can be recognised as such by a more educated public. If you comb the newspapers of the first

half of the 20th century, you'll find almost no mention of unexplained aerial phenomena and if you do, it will probably be of the lightning ball variety which was popular during the inter-war period. There's a simple reason for this: there were hardly any aeroplanes in the world then compared to the number

we have now.
Aviation before WWII was an expensive business which only the rich and the military could indulge in. The fifties brought in the jet age and with it an unprecedented boom in the amount of air traffic seen in our skies across the world. What were country people to make of these noisy, flashing beasts that screamed over their heads? Of course they reported UFO's all the time, heads full of B-movie attackers from Mars. If you don't think that there are that many credulous people out there, think back to when Orson Welles broadcast the radio play of War of the Worlds and

panic gripped the nation. Not all of it of course, but enough to provide more than enough data to prove that there is a sizable minority who will believe anything under the right conditions.

For years, the conditions have been exactly right for belief in such phenomena. Nobody in authority has come out and laid down the position of the state clearly (or rather, they have but no one believes

them). The UK government is still reeling from the revelations of Nick Pope, who has published a book of memoirs on his career with the Ministry of Defence - working as an investigator into UFO's in the strictest meaning of the phrase, he found there was a hard core of a few percent that simply could not be explained away by conventional means - these, he deduced, must therefore be real sightings. However, a few inexplicable things in the sky only proves that there are a few inexplicable things in the sky, not that they are conclusive proof of Alien visitation. The US government, supposedly a big fan of freedom of information, has still failed to come up with any official reason for why it participated in a cover-up at Roswell, because one undeniably did take place. Radio broadcasters were threatened; witnesses intimidated and all evidence confiscated. People at the scene not bound by military codes of secrecy repeatedly tell of miraculous fragments of material, metallic in appearance, which would reform after being crumpled into a ball; thin enough to be folded yet able

to withstand any attempt to further break them up.
Do none of these pieces remain undiscovered? Did the civilians who took some of it not hide even one piece which would corroborate their story?

The 1947 Roswell incident is still held as a talisman for UFO believers. The base commander initially released a report to the local newspaper to the effect that a flying saucer had been recovered, but this was soon retracted as the official story of a downed Radar Target balloon came out. This too was acknowledged as a cover-up for Project Mogul, another balloon-based project designed to spy on the Russian's attempts to manufacture atomic weapons. Only now in 1997, the fiftieth anniversary year, has the Air Force come out with another story: the 'bodies' recovered from the crash site were no more than mannequins, designed to test the effects of a pilot parachuting from extremely high altitudes. Their odd appearance and apparent "mutilation" as seen by witnesses came from a rather nasty landing via a malfunctioning balloon which was supposed to take them into the stratosphere. Perhaps the most convincing reason for the crash site to have excessive amounts of secrecy walled around it is that the time of the event, 1947, was just after the War and the Roswell air base was home to the world's only Atomic Bomber squadron and of the Enola Gaye, which had dropped Fat Boy on Hiroshima. The test site for the solar system's (and possibly this galaxy's) first extra-celestial nuclear explosion was in the same restricted area and the whole base was one of the most secure in the US, if not the world. The atomic bomb was then, as now, the most devastating weapon known to man and was shrouded in secrecy. If there were going to be any covert operations and secret missions with experimental equipment, this was the place to do it. Anti-Communist feelings ran high as the arms race was just about to start (bear in mind that the number of nuclear weapons at that time could have been counted on one hand — the Russians had none that could be used in aggression and the Americans were struggling to make more than the handful they had then). In the eyes of the public, the Roswell base was the Area 51 of it's day and the military leadership saw no reason to discourage this idea. If anything from the base had crashed, it would have been a top priority to stop any information about it getting into the wrong hands — why then attract the attention of the world with the claim that a flying saucer had been found? None of it makes sense. Witnesses give conflicting reports. A recent discovery of an autopsy of what looks like an Alien body has surfaced, but cannot be authenticated. Season 3's 'Jose Chung's "From Outer Space"', with it's tale of pilots dressed as Aliens and Aliens looking like popular entertainment stars, is beginning to look like a factual documentary.

If you're not quite convinced, then look at the two alternatives:
(1) The government has, since 1947 at least (and some say the pre-war broadcast of 'War of the Worlds' was the start, to test the waters), been gearing itself up to announce to the world that the Aliens are here. The eyewitness reports of not only Roswell but possibly the widespread evidence for mass abduction are all true and are a result of the Alien's desires to commit unknown deeds with the citizens of Earth. As for the conspiracy, if there is one, it can therefore only be a) working against the Aliens as per Dark Skies or b) working with them (the X-Files version).

(2) There are no Aliens. The Roswell incident and all other such accounts of UFO's are the result of a) public hysteria and/or b) a deliberate attempt on behalf of secret government organisations to deceive, inveigle and obfuscate. To what ends, we can only guess at.

Do you consider yourself scientifically minded?
Are you a sane and rational Human Being?
Have you ever had an encounter with the paranormal which defies explanation?
Do you believe in the existence of extra-terrestrials?
Do you believe they are here on Earth?

An increasing number of people will have answered 'yes' to all five questions, without realising that the last one makes a mockery of the others. How many times must serious investigators remind people that extraordinary claims require extraordinary evidence? How often must we endure fools who claim that the absence of proof to the contrary does not disprove their pet theories? Believers must prove it's existence — you can't prove a negative. And so far, in over fifty years of intense investigation, speculation and not a little defamation, the entire world has failed to bring to light one piece of tangible evidence of the existence not only of extra-terrestrial intelligence, but any sign of the paranormal powers which charlatans and con-artists claim to possess. You can find any number of blurry photographs and videos which may or may not show UFO's and you won't have to go further than a mile or two in any direction to find a seemingly normal person give you an account of his or her experiences with strangeness. You can switch on the television and find a programme any day of the week giving authentically-produced reports of paranormal occurrences. Look in the papers and you will see in the classified section adverts extolling the virtues of a hundred and one different faith-healers, psychics and spoon-benders who will solve all your spiritual problems in return for a few measly bucks. Can they all be so hideously, blindly, mistakenly, wilfully wrong? Consider the ways of the professional deceiver, the magician. They practice as much as any other artisan to perfect their craft and then parade it in full view, daring the audience to believe

that the minor miracle they have just witnessed is true. The true magician is bound by the codes of his profession not to take advantage of a credulous public by claiming that his powers are anything but an illusion. Siegfried and Roy pull off some amazing stunts with their jungle cats just as David Copperfield does some pretty neat tricks (but stick to Penn & Teller if you like your magic funny). None of these artists will

to be seen with? Do you think it's cool to be associated with men and women who believe parlour tricks give them a link to the spirit world?

It is often the claim of believers that skeptics never see or experience these events because they do not believe in the paranormal, much in the same way that religious followers

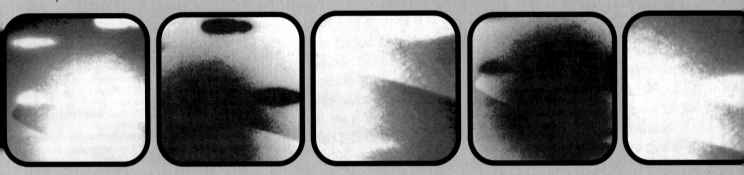

ever claim that they have special powers which enable them to pull off their shows. You will never hear a member of the Magic Circle say that he can save your soul or predict your future (although some precognitive tricks are fairly impressive, no magician has ever got rich by winning the lottery). Why is this, since the effects witnessed in any professional magic show are clearly superior to anything achieved by, say, Israeli cutlery re-shapers?

Because all great magicians are great inventors in the traditional scientific sense. Building on a vast repository of stored information catalogued by former practitioners of the art, it is their job to re-work the old tricks in a modern context and try and come up with some new ones of their own. Do you realise the technical know-how it takes to make a national monument disappear? The physical dexterity required to perform the more dangerous-looking feats of escapology? The concentration needed to pull off a good mind-reading trick? It is not a job for the faint-hearted. Behind it lies an inquiring mind that knows how best to fool his fellow man into thinking what the magician wants him to think. A mind that is versed in a traditional scientific methodology of experimentation and proof. This is the mind-set of the scientist, who knows the value of proper research over hearsay and folk tales. Make a note to yourself next time you're in conversation with someone who claims they were witness to a paranormal event: is this person really the kind you want

will explain the lack of spiritual fulfilment in the infidels lies with their faithlessness. To say that something is as real as the Earth around us (ie ghosts, UFO's, Aliens, psychic powers), and at the same time claim that one needs to believe in them to see them, is ridiculous. You don't believe in teleportation, the destruction and re-integration of household objects or the power of unaided flight (do you?), yet these can be and are performed on television and to live audiences every day in magic shows. You don't have to believe in card tricks to see them happen, which is what makes them so miraculous – for a tiny moment, you can be fooled into thinking the impossible is plausible. The would-be psychics and seance-holders know this and take advantage of Humanity's deep-rooted need to believe in the unknown. We not only want to believe, we need to believe.

Faced with this market niche, it was only a matter of time before a mainstream television company plugged the gap. The X-Files has now successfully muddied the waters of UFO mythology to such an extent that one in ten American citizens believe themselves to have been abducted. Ignoring the fact that this would need an army of UFO's stacked up in a permanent holding pattern over US skies, it is well to remember that statistics can (and are used to) prove anything you like. We know this because our research shows seven out of ten statisticians are liars. Keep an open mind....we want you to think that way.

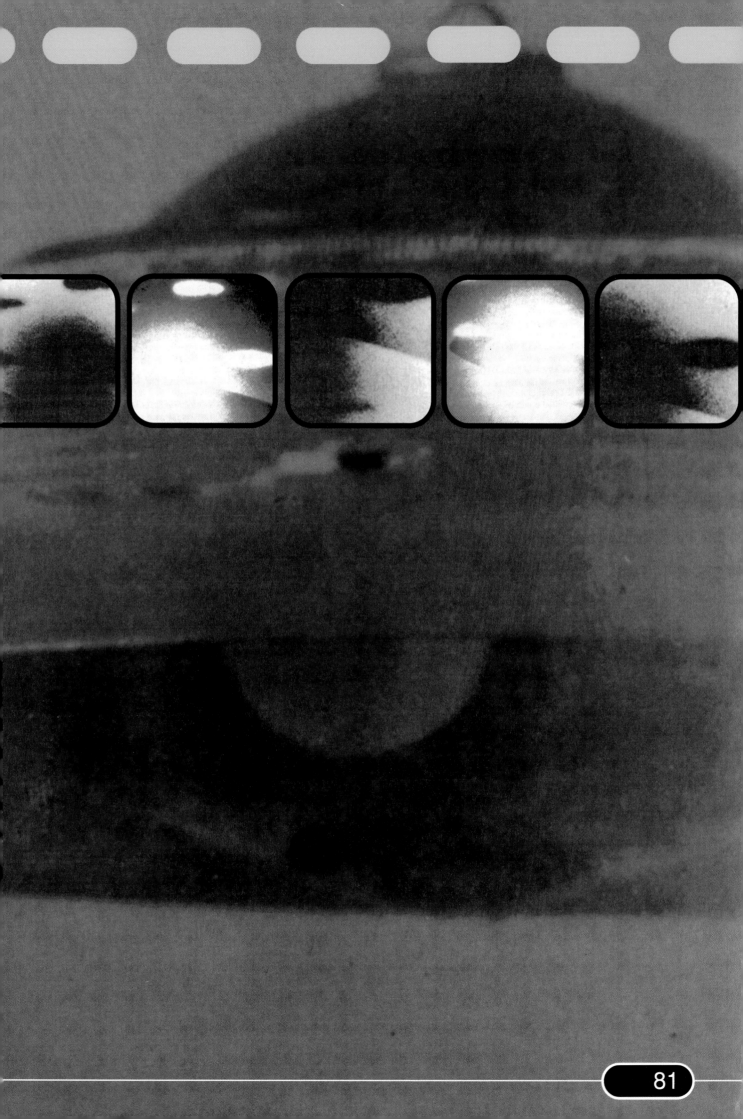

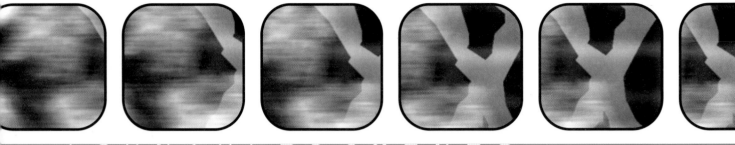

A C K N O W L E D G M E N T S

Company executive - Richard Driscoll.
Arrowhead executive - David Richter.
Design by Daniel Wilkins, illustrations
by Gianfranco Bucci.
Written by Michael Joseph, story by
Ski Newton.
Edited by David Richter.

All photographs in this work are cour-
tesy of Visual Entertainment Archives
Inc. New York U.S.A.